ALSO BY MARY GRIMM

Left to Themselves

STEALING TIME

STEALING TIME

Mary Grimm

RANDOM HOUSE
New York

Some of the stories in this work were originally published in *Beloit
Fiction Journal*, *MSS*, *The New Yorker*, and *Redbook*.

Library of Congress Cataloging-in-Publication Data
Grimm, Mary.
Stealing time / Mary Grimm. — 1st ed.
p.   cm.
ISBN 0-679-40099-0 : $18.00
I. Title.
PS3557.R4933S74   1994
813'.54 — dc20   93-30657

Manufactured in the United States of America on acid-free paper
2   4   6   8   9   7   5   3
First Edition
Book design by Susan Hood

For my first reader,

SUSAN JENNIFER GRIMM DUMBRYS

CONTENTS

STEALING TIME

RESEARCH

At the beginning of my sophomore year of college, I realized that I knew a great deal.

The three months of summer had been like a long dream of being a child again. My parents had moved the summer after I graduated from high school from our house in the city to a suburb of new houses and no sidewalks. When I came back after that first year, I found that my sister and brother, who had spent it in the local high school, were taken up with new friends. My mother was occupied with making the house exactly as she had imagined it before it was built. My father was working.

The whole summer long I did nothing much. I went to the pool — where I knew nobody — and lay on the tiles, scorning a chair, flipping from one side to the other, drinking Cokes. I wandered around the dim, shuttered house, eating my favorite sandwich — American cheese and bologna on white bread with mayonnaise. I was in a sort of trance. I went on dates, at about ten-day intervals, with Andy, my old boyfriend. We never actually went anywhere except to the Valley, a park near his house, where we necked, kissing so passionately and energetically that my lips and tongue would be sore. Nothing else ever happened. With every day that passed, I felt less in control, younger and stupider. I vaguely imagined living with my parents forever, slopping around the house in old clothes, while my brother and sister pursued their vigorous normal lives.

But as soon as I saw my parents driving away from me where I stood in front of the dorm, I snapped out of it. The folds of my new identity draped themselves around me again — not someone's child, not someone's boring older sister. I had a life. I knew people. I had done things.

It all came back to me: how I could go out without telling anyone, how I could smoke in front of adults, how I could stay up as late as I wanted without anyone asking me if I knew what time it was. I was just then trying to become accustomed to the idea that I was a woman. I set it as a task: I would not think of myself as a girl anymore. "Woman," I said to myself, standing there in front of the dorm, "this is the beginning of it," and I saw no irony in the statement.

When I went back upstairs, I found that my roommates and a couple of other girls were making a list of guys that they considered possible. It was our plan to get as many of these guys as we could to ask us out. Some of us were more committed to this than others. Donna Donovan, for instance, was tied up, sort of pre-engaged. Nancy was agreeable to the idea, but it was secondary to her more important objective, which was to get into it with one of the few male professors at our all-girl, nun-ridden school. Julia and I had a further agenda, which we didn't reveal to the others. We wanted to

do it — that is, we wanted to stop being virgins, a wish we
thought was truly unique. So for us the list had other, hidden,
connotations. When a likely name came up, we would look
across the room to signal each other, making small move-
ments with our eyes and mouths, holding in our delight at
our wildness, our cleverness.

I lay across my bed and smoked, blowing the smoke carefully up into the sun-thickened air, listening to them adding
names to the list, and considered the sum total of what I
thought I knew. I believed that I knew how to flirt, that I
knew how to break up with someone, how to conduct myself
in the presence of strange men. I had always known how to
pretend I didn't care about something or someone: not caring
is the refuge and the art of a shy teenager. I knew how to
smoke, how to let someone light my cigarette. I knew how
to sit to make men notice me, how to look up at men from
under my lashes and my bangs so that they felt tall and
powerful. With these things, and good grades, I considered
myself to be prepared for life.

"So how was summer?" Nancy said to me.

"It was deadly."

"What about Andy?" she said, and everyone stopped to
listen.

"He was all right," I said, and paused. "Actually, he was
pretty boring. He seemed awfully young."

"That's the way it is with high school boyfriends," Nancy
said.

"Oh, not Jimmie," Donna Donovan said, and they began
to debate if you could sustain true love over a distance, if you
could be sure when you fell in love in high school that the

guy was the one, when you hadn't seen what the world had to offer in the way of men. We had to stop ourselves from saying "boys" instead of "men."

The truth was that Andy and I had broken up. The truth was that he had come over one night after a longer-than-usual interval and we had, as we always did, gone and gotten hamburgers from the frozen-custard stand, had driven down to the Valley and necked for a while. When we were back at my house, sitting in the car in the driveway, he told me he wanted to break up. There followed a long conversation in which we dissected our relationship and what we had liked about each other and what he liked about the girl he was breaking up with me for, Darlene. We had been remarkably frank, even more remarkable if you considered the fact that we had never had a conversation before at all. It turned out that Darlene looked something like me — brown hair, brown eyes, tall. She was more developed, he said. I took this in good part, because I had a horror of becoming more developed. It turned out that he had been seeing Darlene for more than a year.

"You were seeing her when we were going out last summer?" I said.

"Well, yeah," he said, fiddling with the car keys.

I thought I ought to be mad. "I ought to be mad," I said.

"Are you?" he asked.

"No. Is she sexier than me?"

"Maybe," he said.

"What does that mean?"

"I guess it means yes."

"Well, in what way is she?"

But here he stuck, unable to say how she was sexier than

me. They had done other things, he said, other things than
kissing. I was fascinated, on the edge of my seat. What things?
I wanted to ask. He said he didn't think of me that way.

"But then why did you ever go out with me?" I said.

"Well, there was something about you."

"What?"

"I don't know. Something."

I really wanted to know. It never occurred to me then that
he had gone out with me for the same reason that I had gone
out with him: because I was safe, because I was good practice.
We had been nice to each other, although we didn't know
each other at all. We had gotten to be good, maybe even
great, kissers.

I had been depressed for a couple of days. He was only my
second boyfriend, and one of the only three boys I'd ever
dated, and one of those three had been someone my mother
had made me invite to the prom, the son of a friend of hers.
Thanks to Joey Skrovan I had a picture of myself in a long
white flouncy strapless dress with matching chiffon stole to
take out and look at when I was old.

But I didn't mention any of this to the other girls. I had
made Andy more interesting than he was, and for that reason
I now had to pretend that I was more upset than I felt.

"It was just fate," I said. "We grew apart." I thought that
bringing fate into it sounded very worldly, almost jaded.

"You can't expect to form a lifetime relationship in high
school," Nancy said.

"You're better off without him if he was so fickle," Donna
Donovan said.

Julia said nothing. She looked at me consideringly, and I
knew that she suspected my explanation. I shrugged to con-

firm her guess, and as a promise that I would tell her about it later.

The list lay on the floor. We forgot about it, telling stories about the summer. Everyone's parents had been impossible in varying degrees. Everyone's old friends had been unsatisfactory. We had all been bored, we said, except Donna Donovan, who had been a counselor at an ecumenical camp where she had learned a lot and grown in Christian love. We let her tell us about the masses held outside by the lake and the prayer trail, but when she got to how the chaplain had done laying on of the hands as part of the Spiritual Search and Growth Workshop, it was too much for us, and we started to make dirty jokes. We loved Donna, but we considered it to be our duty to make her more real. She was miffed and retired to the bathroom to wash and set her hair, but we knew she wouldn't be gone for long, she would forgive us.

After she left, the conversation got more graphic and more personal. I believed then that all of us were virgins, and the talk honored this convention. But we went as far as we could, given this limitation. I felt able to make a pretty respectable contribution, even though Andy and I had never done anything but kiss. I had last year at college under my belt, so to speak, when one guy ("guys" was what we said when it seemed too unbearably silly to say "men") had tried to get his hand inside my panty girdle, and I had allowed another to unhook my bra. I had seen a busboy in his underpants, at the cafeteria where I worked. I made as much of all this as I could.

I took the list with me when Julia and I went off to her room. She was sharing a double with a senior. She explained

the advantage of this to me: the senior had a key. Perhaps
she could be persuaded to lend it. We could stay out past
curfew. I liked the idea of staying out, but not the idea of the
key. I imagined coming back at three or four in the morning,
unlocking the door and stepping into the dimly lit lobby
of our dorm, straight into the arms of Miss Trudell, our
housemother. She was a silent woman who had a graduate
degree in Phys. Ed., so burdened with her huge ruddy arms
and legs that she seemed barely able to move. Her face, too,
was immobile, all horizontal, her mouth and eyes straight
lines under the dense thatch of her hair. I was afraid of her,
not so much of what she would do, but just of her being what
she was in the same world that I lived in, struggling.

"We could go down the back stairs," I said. "Patricia told
me they're all open from this side and there's a door at the
bottom that opens out at the back of the building. Then
you're not signed out. No one even knows you're gone. You
just can't get back in."

We considered this. The first question was whether it was
reliable. Patricia Lee was a mine of information, most of it
having to do with men and the wiles needed to entrap them.
She was Chinese, a junior. She seemed years older than anyone else there. Her flat Oriental features were placid, the
folds and curves of her gold skin made me want to touch
them, trace them with my fingers. She liked to give us advice,
Julia and I, and we loved to hear it, for she was so cynical, so
practical. Some of the things she said made no sense to me,
but I liked them. She had told us last year, right in the middle
of the hall, that we should get an undergarment called a
"merry widow." This was to protect our virtue.

"They put their hands in but it is no good. It is all the same" — she indicated with her hands a wall from chest to crotch — "from here to here. That stops them."

"It sounds awful," Julia said. "Isn't it uncomfortable?"

Patricia shrugged. "You can get it trimmed with lace. Black. They call you a tease, but they like it."

Even then I had had doubts about whether I wanted my virtue protected, but I didn't air them in the hall.

"What did Patricia say about the stairs?" Julia asked now.

"She said she uses them when she wants to stay out all night. Then she comes back in the morning, so it's just like she went out early." She had said that she used the stairs mostly on Saturday night, taking care to wear her good coat over her date clothes and, I guess, her merry widow. In the coat, with a chiffon scarf tied over her shiny black hair, she would purse her lips devoutly as she came in, playing the part of one who had attended early mass.

We both thought about the idea of staying out all night. Where would we go? Who would we be with?

"We could find out right now if it would work," I said.

We left Julia's room and strolled casually down to the other end of the hall where the laundry and TV room was. I looked into it. There was one girl sitting with her back against the radiator, reading while her wash whirled and sloshed. The double doors that led to the stairs were right next to the laundry-room door. Julia stood with her hand on the knob. Silently we gestured to each other — she would go down and I would stay by the door as lookout. She took off her shoes, gave them to me, and slid through.

It was hard to be standing there with no excuse, holding a pair of shoes. It was a quiet time, when we were supposed to be studying, or anyway not making noise. But no one had any homework yet, so girls were visiting back and forth between rooms, trying on each other's new clothes, looking at pictures of new boyfriends or engagement rings, exchanging stories about summer jobs. I put Julia's shoes on the floor. Every once in a while someone came out in the hall and I tried to look as if I was waiting for something. I stooped down to make it seem as if I was fixing my sock. I leaned against the doorjamb of the laundry room, but the girl inside looked curiously at me. Finally, I merely stood. I saw Miss Trudell come out of her suite at the other end of the hall. I waited for her to lumber toward me, but she simply got on the elevator and disappeared. "She wouldn't be so fat if she took the stairs," I thought.

It seemed like a very long time before Julia tapped on the door. I opened it and we ran, snorting with laughter, Julia in her socks, me clumping along behind her. When we got to her room, her senior roommate was there. She looked at us with amazement as we rolled around on the bed and the floor, laughing and hitting each other. She raised her eyebrows, but smiled at us, and putting her finger in her book to mark her place, got up and left, saying she would be in the lounge if anyone wanted her.

"We did it, we did it, we did it," I said. "You did it."

"It was easy," Julia said. She lowered her voice. "You just go down, down, down. I bent over when I went past the doors. I looked out at the bottom. It was right by the garbage cans. I can't think why we never noticed it before."

We felt wonderful. We fished the list out from under the bed, and spent the hour before dinner adding to it, planning which guys we would stay out with all night, which ones would be the most difficult, which were the best-looking. When we went down to dinner, we were so sick with laughing that we could hardly eat.

But we forgot about all that, really, for the next month. I don't know what happened to the list. We never saw it again. We were taken up with our classes, and we started to go downtown to the Loop, taking the El, which we hadn't done the year before. I began the habit of taking long walks with Nancy all over Chicago's North Side, where our college was, during which we talked about our future careers. I was most serious with Nancy. She was going to be a doctor. I vacillated. Every avenue seemed tainted to me. My mother thought I was going to be a teacher, but I did not want to be like the teachers I had known, who were either nuns or lay teachers who were odd in some way. Being a doctor was gruesome. Being a lawyer sounded boring. Even if I wanted to do what my father and my uncles had done, which was work in the steel industry, this was closed to me. I was a girl, and the first girl in my family to go to college, and it was my duty to look to better things. It is strange that, interested as I was in sex, I never considered just getting married.

I started going out with Ben Ehrenberg, the roommate of one of Nancy's boyfriends. He was half Jewish, which I found exotic. He had told me this when we first met as if he expected me to sneer or turn away, but, a Catholic from a densely Catholic city, I had never even met a Jew before. I only knew about anti-Semitism from books, and because I had read about it I thought it was something that was all over and done with. I found his defensiveness, his chip, disarming. We would go out to a movie or to eat, and then back to his apartment, which he shared with a fraternity brother. We

would lie on his bed fully clothed. We would kiss every once
in a while. I already knew that he didn't turn me on. This
was something about which I was newly expert, for it had
happened to me a month before, dancing with a stranger at
an IIT mixer. It was not the first time I had slow-danced, but
it was the first time that I had been held so close by someone
I physically liked, my chest against his chest, my stomach
against his, his leg pressed between my legs, his hand solidly
on my back. I was wearing a dress made of some thin crepe
material — very demure, a little bow at the neck — but no
protection, no barrier to what passed between our skins.
When I felt him rising against my body, and my own spreading heat, the pressure, the opening, I knew what it was. I
didn't feel this with Ben.

But there were things I liked about him. I liked the fact
that he talked a lot, since it meant that I didn't have to, and
I liked the things he talked about, for he liked books and
plays, and had an attachment to them that was made even
more intense by the business degree that was in his future. I
liked his articulate, aggressive intentions toward me. It was
flattering to be so unmistakably wanted.

On our third date, he brought up the question of sex — did
I want to? He didn't have the finesse or deceitfulness to
suggest that it was a question of love. It was accepted that he
liked me a lot, and that I liked him well enough. It wasn't
love that he was pushing, but experience. He, too, wanted
to do it.

"My father told me I ought to get laid," he said, sitting in
his car, one of us on either side of the gear shift listening to
Johnny Mathis. He had been trying to teach me to shift so
that I could sit right up next to him while he drove one-

handed. I wasn't getting it, possibly because I didn't like sitting that way. I liked sitting next to the window, where I could look out if I wanted to, or look over at him and appreciate the strange fact of this male in a car with me, our bodies moving through space and time, just us knowing where we were, the dark and the lights moving past. I hadn't had so many dates that I'd gotten used to this yet.

"Your father said that to you?" I couldn't believe that anyone's father would encourage him to have sex. "Weren't you embarrassed?"

"Yeah, a little. But he's a pretty great guy. He said it'd be good for me."

I didn't like the idea of myself as a sexual vitamin, but I was interested in this sort of parent, so unlike my own, who had never discussed sex with me at all, much less recommended it. "What does he look like?" I asked.

"Oh, you know. He looks pretty good for his age, I guess."

"How old is he?"

"Forty-two."

Younger than my parents, but still old. When we got to his apartment, I went to the bookcase by the TV to look at the family picture: Ben, his parents, his two little sisters. Ben looked more like his mother, I saw. He had her solidness, her light coloring, their hands fell awkwardly away from their bodies at the same angle. His father was darker, more at ease in the shape of his face, where he was most like Ben. He looked right at the camera, smiling.

I let Ben take all my clothes off that night. He removed them one by one, fumbling with the buttons of my skirt and the fastening of my bra. I was very cool during this, watching him, watching myself. I waited for a sign. I liked the novel sensation of the roughness of the upholstery against my thighs as I sat on the ottoman smoking a cigarette, but my body was inert. I wouldn't let Ben touch me, and I wouldn't let him take his clothes off.

I didn't go out with him for a while after that, though Nancy pressed me to double with her and Charles. I started hanging out with a group who came to the college coffee-house in the evenings, talkers and guitar players, tossing back the stray locks of their hair as they stirred more Cremora into their coffee. Julia and I inherited the management of this coffeehouse from her senior roommate. The profit we made from selling the coffee and pop and pretzels was to go to the missions, the same place we had sent our outgrown clothes and used books, our saved-up candy-bar money, and hundreds of homemade rosaries that we learned to knot with a special needle in high school — so ugly that I felt guilty to think of anyone having to use them. I imagined the knots hard and unforgiving against their black fingers, the snaky cords the color of dried mustard.

I was very interested in these guitar players, these singers of folk songs. I watched them pick through the records stacked up on the deep window ledge. I studied their moves while I poured their refills. I let my fingers touch theirs when I took their money and gave them back their change, savoring that dry slide of fingertips against palm, as overstimulating as the dark reheated coffee swirling in their cups. After we closed, Julia and I would wash the cups and stack the records, sweep up the pretzel crumbs, arrange the chairs around the tables, talking all the while about one or another of them.

The first time I stayed out all night I didn't use the stairs. I left at eight-thirty, a respectable time, with Julia. It was not a coffeehouse night. We were going with two of the guitar players to the apartment of a friend of theirs to play pinochle. More and more people showed up as the night went on, and the pinochle game divided and reproduced itself into two, plus a bridge game, and a big sprawling game of hearts. By midnight we were all playing hearts, with three decks. There was some beer in the kitchen, but almost everyone was drinking Dr Pepper or cream soda or Coke. It was hot with the kind of heat that you feel in steam-heated apartments in the winter, it pressed on you, it was tropical. At one point some of us had been playing strip acey-deucey, and we had not bothered to put on the clothes we had surrendered. I had lost a hair bow, my shoes, and my blouse, all of which I could see, if I turned my head, laid out neatly on a chair by the radiator.

"We ought to be going back," Julia said to me.

"I guess."

The guy sitting next to me turned and said, "You don't have to go yet, do you?" He kept his eyes on a level with mine, avoiding any angle that would show him to be looking at the line of my slip against my skin, or the crisscrossed arrangement of the two sets of straps — slip and bra — on my shoulders. He had lost his watch. He was shoeless, shirtless. I had spent some time that night looking out of the corner of my eye at the smooth, nearly hairless planes of his chest.

"We do have to, though," I said to him. His name was John and I said it silently, using just my tongue, not moving my lips, feeling the O inside my mouth like a piece of hard candy. "Would you pass me the pretzels?" I said, so that I could watch how his skin moved over his muscles when he

reached across the floor. I started to explain to him the sign-
out system, looking all the while into his eyes, sucking the
salt off the pretzel I had chosen, appealing to Julia for details
or confirmation.

"So when you signed out, did you write in you were going
to some guy's apartment?" he asked Julia.

"Well, no," she said. "I couldn't think what to put."

"So what'd you do?" I asked her.

She leaned across the floor and grabbing the back of my
neck, pulled my ear to her mouth. "I didn't sign out," she
said, her voice breathy in my hair.

"You didn't?" I said. We looked at each other, thinking
the same thought.

It was so easy, much easier than the stairs would have been.

After the first time, we did it fairly often — once or twice
a week — but with a randomness that we calculated with the
caution of spies. The feeling of walking through the lobby
and away from the building, unsigned out, illicit, was delicious, like silk against our skins. The air, the wind, the yellow
gleam of the streetlight were witness to our lawlessness. The
look of the curving metal arm and the transparent fruit of the
globe hanging over my head as I walked in as from an early
class could make my breath catch in my throat.

We played cards, took early-morning walks, sent out for
pizza and meatball sandwiches at 2:00 A.M. We almost always
stayed at that same apartment, which was a sort of clubhouse
for a shifting group of college kids. Three guys from Loyola
paid the rent, but sometimes none of them were there. No
one slept in beds, hardly anyone ever slept at all. Sleeping
was not the point, not the literal variety, nor the euphemism-

for-sex type, though I knew that this was what anyone would think if Julia and I had said what we were doing. John and I were moving slowly closer to each other, but we hadn't done much more than kiss a month later when the rumor went around at school that the honor sign-out system was being abused.

Julia heard about this in her political science class. "We'd better lay off for a while," she said that night at the coffee-house. We were in the back, layering paper napkins in the pretzel baskets.

"There's that party this Friday," I said. This was to be an all-night poker game. Tequila had been promised. "I've never had tequila," I said.

"It's got a worm in the bottom," Julia said.

It would be stupid, we decided, and so when Nancy came in later that night and said did I want to go out with Ben and Charles on Friday, I said yes. Julia decided to go to the movies with her senior roommate.

Ben still wanted to have sex. We were at his apartment, Nancy and Charles and I, and it seemed very quiet after the noise and sweat of the dance at their fraternity. Nancy and Charles were sitting on the couch. I sat with my feet tucked under the circle of my skirt spread out around me on the floor. Every once in a while I patted it with my hands to feel the nice springiness of the crisp petticoats under it. Ben rushed around making drinks, changing records on the stereo, and playing with the sound level. We were drinking Tom Collinses, which I had never had before. They were a summer drink, I gathered from what the others said, and so it was somehow racy to be drinking them now, in December. I

began to feel larger but lighter. I could imagine that I might
leap into the air and the fluffy layers of my skirt and petticoats
would support me like a parachute.

The others were talking about drinking they'd done, in
high school and more recently. I was not a great drinker and
so had nothing to contribute, but I wanted to be a part of the
adult atmosphere. I sucked some more Tom Collins and got
a cigarette, which I held for Ben to light. "Too bad we signed
out tonight," I said to Nancy.

"What do you mean?" she asked.

"I mean if we hadn't signed out, we wouldn't have to go
back."

"Not go back?" Charles said.

I remembered then that Julia and I had agreed not to tell
anyone, and I thought for a minute of pretending that this
was something I'd just thought of, a whim, a brainwave. But
I could see that Nancy, whose sophistication and worldliness
I so admired, had never dreamed of doing anything like this.
So I told them all about it – the nonchalant walks out past
the desk, the smoky card games, the great crowd we hung
out with. I brought John's name up casually, because he
was good-looking and Nancy knew who he was. I gave the
impression, as well as I could, of hordes of men who waited
to hear what I would say, waited to light my cigarettes,
poured my drinks. I even mentioned the tequila I'd given up
that night.

The effect was not what I'd hoped. Nancy looked thought-
ful, Charles concerned in a fatherly way, from the vantage of
his status as senior. Ben was plainly agitated. I was relieved
when Nancy changed the subject to next week's snow carni-

val. About twenty minutes later, Nancy and Charles went into the bedroom with their usual excuse, that they were going to look at Charles's photos of sunsets. Ben was in the kitchenette. I went over to the stereo to look for a more exciting record than Johnny Mathis. Ben came up behind me, and I turned to him, holding an empty record jacket.

"Have you got something by The Association?" I asked him.

For answer, he flung his arms around me, pinning me against the wall, kissing me, crushing me. I could smell the toothpaste on his breath. He must have been brushing his teeth in the kitchen, I thought, as I tried to push him off. I wriggled and twisted and finally pulled out from underneath and stepped away. "Ben," I said, and then I saw that he had taken off his pants. I could see them in the kitchen, neatly hung over the back of a chair. He was wearing boxer shorts that looked remarkably like my father's, and I smiled.

He was breathing hard, and he didn't smile back. Johnny Mathis was singing. Ben was looking at me out of little hard eyes. I should call Nancy and Charles? Just casually, just to ask if they wanted to hear Johnny Mathis one more time or something faster? I should do what Chinese Patricia had recommended if you had neglected to wear your merry widow? You kick them in between the legs, she said. I should say I would tell his father, whose picture I could see on the shelf over the TV, his father, his mother, his little sisters, hands folded in their laps? I should say O.K.? Wasn't this what I wanted anyway, to have it over with, behind me?

He crossed the room and took me by the arms. I owe it to him, I thought. I'm here. There was a sort of symmetry that demanded my participation, Charles and Nancy in the bedroom, Ben and I in the living room. "What if we have another drink first?" I said.

He kissed me again, hard enough to hurt my lips with his teeth, and without thinking further I screamed as loud as I'd ever heard anyone scream, I pulled his hair with my free hand and when he put his mouth over mine again I bit his tongue and his lip, and when he pulled away from me I hit him, I grabbed a stack of records and threw them at him, clumsily splaying them over the floor. When Nancy and Charles appeared at the bedroom door, I picked up his chemistry book and I hit him on the head with it until Nancy and Charles separated us.

It was more than three months later, in the spring, that I finally did it, not with Ben, of course. There was a song that was very popular then, that went on and on, had a six-minute version in fact, and it was that song, I am convinced, that was responsible for my marriage, my pregnancy, and everything that happened after. There was a part in that song toward the end where the music took a little turn back on itself and started at the beginning again, as if the musicians had had enough and wanted to wind it up. It gave you an inevitable sort of feeling, futile and filled with a lost emotion. I seem to remember saying "Oh, well" to myself and turning to John, who was pressed up against me on the couch, and giving myself over to him mentally. There was a wonderful sort of feeling, a wave of desire washing over me that had not so much to do with sex or even with John, but with a desire to make solid, to objectify the dark emotions in the music, a longing for change, for an opening up, for the future. And it was wonderful in a way, to have the means of change there close to hand, and not used up or soiled by consequences as they are when you are older. The air in my lungs was sharp, painful and exciting, like smoking for the first time. I did it as casually and easily as shedding a skin or growing out of a dress. It hurt a little, but the stain of blood was so small, a thread only, dark red on the badly laundered sheet, that in a way it hardly seemed to have happened at all.

WE WHO ARE YOUNG

::

This is on a day four days before the dead middle of summer, heavy with heat, flowers opening from the pressure of their own fertility, dogs panting, children demanding the sprinkler.

"Aunt Sylvia is staying over with your uncle Jim Connors," Mother says, "and it would be nice if you went to see her. We went yesterday and she said how nice it would be to see you all, her dear brother Richard's girls." We have eaten too much dinner, so unlike any dinners that Kate and I are likely to make at home, a dinner that only your mother would make when her children and her grandchildren come over on Sunday. Too much gravy, too many white floury rolls with butter, too many pieces of pie with syrup-glazed fruit oozing from its sugared crust. The promise of activity is daunting.

But Mother goes on (noting, no doubt, our sighs, our inert, reluctant bodies). "She's over eighty, if you remember. Who knows if she'll make it back this way to visit again." And, knowing this is true, feeling the weight and the duty of all her eighty-one years (or eighty-two?), we nod, we agree. We will go and see Aunt Sylvia, we will fall into our roles as nieces, as great-nieces.

We: Richard's girls — me (Markie) and Kate; Kate's daughters — Claudia and Vicky. Kate's husband, Dak, will come later because he is not a social person, and she is not his aunt, after all. He'll take his time — he may want another piece of pie.

"Don't walk," says Mother. "Take the car, it's so dusty."

But no, we say — we always walk there. It takes only fifteen minutes. Half an hour at the most.

"It's too hot," Mother says. "Wear hats. Keep to the shady side. Your father will follow in the car and you can flag him down when he passes. Let me lend you some suntan lotion. Are you wearing good walking shoes?"

It is hot, really hot — sweat drips from our noses, the tips of our bangs, and quivers in the short hairs that shine gold on Claudia's neck. Kate and I would walk this way to see the Connors cousins when we used to hang out with them, on long hot summer days, when we were too young to have jobs, when we were boyfriendless teenagers (except for our cousin Ricky, who was girlfriendless), when we had nothing to do for long long stretches, such unimaginable stretches of empty unfilled time.

Everything was so slow: we could look into a mirror then, at our hair, at the unsatisfactory shape of our lips, at the mysterious expression of our eyes when we were thinking about certain things — and when we came out of that long dream only an hour had gone by. Sometimes to escape all this we would walk the mile and a half to the Connors' house. The Connors cousins felt these things too, but when we were together the nameless feelings would be spread out, dissipated through the five of us, so that we were eased.

What did we do? We drank Cokes at a long wood table. We lay on the couch or in the lawn chairs or on the cold linoleum floor. We played records in the basement, where it was cool, putting them on the old record player that played at varying speeds — now a little too fast, now a little too slow. We went into the wild part back of the house and lay on the long grass in a triangular space between three trees that stretched up beyond the second growth of the newer woods, and smoked — marijuana once, that Ricky had gotten from a sailor at the bus station downtown — "Take it," he'd said to Ricky, hitching up his duffel bag, "they'll just find it on me back at the base."

We used to take the back way to the park to go rock-climbing — this was a good thing, the best thing, because it was hard. The rocks were not a jungle gym, not meant to be climbed, they were just there, and they used up that energy and torpor that we could feel through all our bodies, that slowed and tensed our muscles. Sometimes we went to a different part of the park, where there were no rocks, and it was so featureless that we could pretend we were lost.

But now, when we get to their house, they, the cousins, all are gone, physically in their present selves, as well as in their dearly loved past selves. One is working overtime at her job in insurance. One is married and living in Oregon. One now is dead. Only Uncle Jim Connors, our father's brother, is there, and his wife, our Aunt Betty, and Aunt Sylvia, who wanted so much to see us.

We all sit down: Uncle Jim Connors in the chair by the

fireplace, Aunt Sylvia on the couch between Claudia and me.
Kate sits on the end of one of the long wooden benches by
the table, just under the phone, where sometimes we used
to call up boys who we hoped might be but never were our
boyfriends. Our father sits in the wooden rocker that was his
own father's. Vicky sits in the chair that Ricky (who now is
dead) always sat in — the captain's chair by the window from
which you could lean out and see your reflection in the pond.

What can we talk about? Coffee? Orange juice? A little gin
and Squirt? Is it too hot? Is the air conditioning high enough?
How is our mother feeling in this heat? Did we notice the
height of the corn at the fork of the road?

No one says, "Oh, Aunt Sylvia, you look so old, your skin
is stretched so tight over your temples and your jaw — how
can you be alive?"

We are afraid to touch her and as afraid to say anything to
her, for if we speak of the real things of our lives they would
be like bruises, intrusions — our work, our lovers, our cars and
washers that need to be fixed. And what else is there? But
we try: the loveliness of Kate's children, Claudia and Vicky,
their schoolwork, their hair. This is in the right direction —
to the future. And the past — Aunt Sylvia's life as a teacher:
how she taught grades one through six, sometimes all at the
same time, how she never whipped anyone, how she made
the bad boys chop wood.

But this, the present? We are saying good-bye in these little
bits and pieces of foreseen and remembered time. When we
all rode Aunt Sylvia's neighbor's horse, except it threw Kate
on its way to the barn. When I got burrs in my hair, playing
in the field with the little boy who lived down the road from
Aunt Sylvia's house and they thought my hair would all have

to be cut off, but Aunt Sylvia combed and combed until it was as smooth as ribbons. When Claudia was a baby and had no hair and Kate took her out to see Aunt Sylvia at the farm and she ate one of Aunt Sylvia's own dill pickles at five months old and loved it.

And then our uncle and father tell older stories: about when Richard, our father, was a boy and stole the ice cream from the back step that was meant for the Ladies' Aid. When the girls, their sisters Sylvia and the beautiful Louisa, ate cocoa dry from the box and threw up out their bedroom window so their mother wouldn't know. A question comes up about Louisa's trailer in Florida — did she have it five years? Ten? Didn't she lend it to their cousin for his honeymoon? Yes, but that was in '58. Many of these people are dead, but I think of them standing silent in the room with us, straight and still. They listen and smile. They know how long Louisa had her trailer, but they're not saying.

Aunt Sylvia speaks. She is eighty-one, she says. She will be eighty-two in four months. "I taught school for twenty-seven and a half years," she says. The half year was when she had a heart attack and retired, so as not to have another in front of the children. She says about her husband that he loved his pipe, that he loved to read and smoke on summer evenings like this one, sitting on the porch glider. Her husband is from so long ago that we cannot remember even the color of his hair.

But now we feel quite giddy with the success of our visit. Claudia and Vicky sip their Cokes, Kate and I stir and swirl our coffee cheerfully. Only when Aunt Sylvia gets up to put away her cup and saucer do we feel uneasy. Everyone leans forward, in case one of the bones we can count under her skin should give way. Uncle Jim Connors tells a joke to cover our concern, about what one of the grandkids said about spinach. Children don't like vegetables, we answer. Except carrots, sometimes, and maybe peas, but never turnips or spinach.

"Though Ricky liked spinach," Aunt Betty says.

"He never," says Uncle Jim Connors.

"Why, he did too," she says.

"You know the last thing Ricky wrote me?" Uncle Jim Connors says.

Aunt Betty leaves the room, pretending that she has to tidy up a little, has to go to the bathroom, needs a Kleenex.

Uncle Jim Connors leans forward. "He wrote me what his flight instructor said about how when birds are scared sometimes they fold up their wings" — he demonstrates with his arms — "and drop like a rock and you have to watch because sometimes they drop right into the plane engine. Isn't that the damnedest thing?"

We sit in silence, receiving this story, witnessing the fact that Ricky is dead now these many years, shot down in the jungle, his twisted body brought home some number of missing years later.

Aunt Sylvia shakes her head. She thinks how the last thing her husband said to her was a swear word. She doesn't hold it against him.

Claudia and Vicky are restive, and when Dak finally arrives they jump up and attach themselves to his very solid body. "How about some ice cream," he says, "on a hot day like this?"

"Ice cream!" Claudia and Vicky shout as if they were much younger than they are. But where can it be got — on a Sunday when the store down the road is closed? Like a magician, Dak produces it from just outside the door, a gallon of strawberry.

We will eat it outside, by the pond, in the shade of the willow branches, and there is a lot to do, finding dishes, clean spoons, enough lawn chairs. Aunt Sylvia says she wishes to sit so that her legs are stretched in the sun and we have a bad moment when she insists on moving the chair to the right spot by herself, pulling it by fractions of inches over the rough grass.

"And what grade are you in now?" she asks Claudia, who is in seventh grade, and so rounded, blushing, healthy, so trustingly embellished with eye shadow and lip gloss that she is painful to look at.

"And do you and your sister get along?" she asks.

Claudia nods her head, keeping back all the older-sister things she does to Vicky, all the younger-sister things that Vicky does to get even.

"That's fine," Aunt Sylvia says. "That's the truest kind of love, the love between sisters. It's what lasts the longest." She remembers now, but does not mention, standing in a field in another hot summer long ago, wearing a cotton dress with a small blue flower print and feeling such a pain in her heart because she was not as pretty as her sister Louisa — the beautiful Louisa, as beautiful as the day, who is only a photograph now and a memory of hurt and desire. Sylvia stood there and wished to be dead with a powerful spell-casting wish, but she continued to feel her dress blow against her body and the pinch of her metal-rimmed glasses — she continued to live.

Now, with this memory filling her mind, the hot wind blowing her thin gray hair away from her face, she looks at

Claudia and Vicky, marveling at their youth, and she eats her strawberry ice cream, a milky pink that is the same color as her cardigan sweater. Are these Richard's daughters, too? she wonders. She doesn't ask, doesn't want to hurt their feelings. She doesn't want them to know that she has forgotten. Here we are in the present, she thinks, but not everyone has come this far.

BOOK OF DREAMS

::

Of course we asked for a pony. Of course we said we would keep it in the garage. Ours was the sort of family where we didn't get one. We had matching transistor radios, bikes, red wagons, a dollhouse with attached garage and tiny electric lights. But no pony. Between us, Kate and I had sixty-eight dolls. I had four more than she did, but I was older.

Kate and I are well aware of the rap we take for having been spoiled, but can you blame us because our parents loved us? Our friends have said to other friends that we are too close. They keep telling us they envy us, but among themselves they insist on the natural order of things: jealousy and rivalry between siblings, fights to the death over comic books and memories and the family silver. We did fight some-times — what to name the pony was one thing, back when we still thought we might get one if we were very, very good. I wanted to name it Whitey. Kate wanted to name it after her imaginary friend, Janet Lee. We fought over it for weeks, whenever our parents weren't around. When Christmas came it was almost a relief to get the dollhouse instead.

Later we fought because of Len. This was 1968 and we lived in Cleveland; I was seventeen, and Kate was two years younger. It was just a matter of a few months, maybe a year, when I spent all my time with him and hardly any with Kate. After the first flush of sex and romance, it was back to reality, and I even thought then that we might discuss this particular fight, Kate and I, someday.

I met Len in a bar and I absolutely did not know when I met him that he was a musician. He had a glow, of course — a sheen of difficulty. A look of being just what you shouldn't have. He looked too bad to be true. I worked in a bank that first summer, and I went over to his house after work as often as I could. I rode on the bus and walked six blocks to get there, still in my teller's uniform: a royal-blue straight skirt and bolero jacket. With my skirt blue and smooth over my hips and with nothing under the jacket except underwear, partly because it was hot (this was my excuse) and partly because I was young and wanted to feel loose in my clothes, I sat and drank Coke on the floor while he restrung his guitar. Or I smoked cigarettes on the upstairs back porch while he leaned on the railing and fingered over the hard parts. I played pinochle and hearts with the other guys in the band. It was heaven. I remembered thinking once that I would give my life to stay overnight, which I couldn't do, of course, because of my parents — because I was seventeen and lived at home.

But being around Len was also very ordinary, in a good way. It was like anybody else's teenage life. We went to movies. We smoked cigarettes and ate hamburgers. We necked. We went all the way.

During what should have been the winter of my junior year in college Len and I got married. Then — almost right away — it turned out that marriage was more like *I Love Lucy* than like every little girl's dream of being one-and-only to the lead singer in a bar band. You're the wife of a musician: Oh, boy! He's home all day! He brings his band to play for the scholarship benefit when you nag him! He forgets to introduce you to minor celebrities! Still, secretly, I thought Kate — and certainly our cousin Carol Ann — ought to envy me, but tactfully I kept this to myself.

Carol Ann's life was dull just then: no good men, a job in a library where everyone was twenty years older than she was — a far cry from when we were little and she held all the cards. Back then, Carol Ann sometimes knew what would happen before it did. She would dream it. These were documented dreams kept faithfully in a book that contained the minutes of our Dream Club, a dead secret between Kate, me, and Carol Ann. (She had to be Karol Ann in the Dream Club, because it was agreed for some reason that we all had to have a K in our names: Kate, Karol Ann, and Markie, which was my name then because of Carol Ann's little brother's inability to say my real name, Margaret.) The club was formed after Kate and I found out about Carol Ann's ability, which as far as she knew she had always had. We thought (perhaps just I thought) that with practice we might develop similar talents, but try as we would to favorably interpret dream objects and ensuing events, Kate's and my dreams were always about Jell-O–filled swimming pools and forgetting our underwear.

Our records showed conclusively that Carol Ann was the only one who could do it. If she dreamed a red wagon that had been filled with dirt by the boys down the street, someone would spot a red wagon filled with dirt. If she predicted a plaid dress for Kate, it would appear. But the problem was, we would never know when the predicted things would happen. (The plaid dress didn't show up until Kate's birthday three years later.) Mostly they were such ordinary, even such boring things that it didn't matter. What difference did it make that our uncle would buy new windshield wipers for his car and lose one on the way home, as he did two weeks after Carol Ann dreamed it? It was just a thing, a part of life — something we might talk about when we were away from adults. By the time we were interested in boyfriends — when dream previews might have done us some good — she no longer dreamed true. And, to be honest about it, there were some leftover dreams that never happened and were never accounted for.

Of course she missed the other way, too — things happened that she did not dream. I mean, how could she have dreamed Len's death? And if she had, what would she have made of it? How could she have dreamed the ambulance — the moment when, sitting in front on the way to the hospital, I put my hand on the dashboard as we swung around the corner at the end of our block and felt the dust slide under my fingers; dreamed a small bit of matter moving, red on red, up an artery, traveling brainward; dreamed his white hand that lay unmoving on the rough white sheet; dreamed that I had to pick it up, had to hold it, while the nurses, all in white, stood watching? No.

I myself had a dream, later, in New York, in 1978 — this was two years after Len's death, maybe fifteen years after the last meeting of the Dream Club. I was there for Carol Ann's marriage to Simon. I went alone, although I had expected to travel with Kate. But I'll get to the dream later.

It was bumpy on the way from Cleveland — a little scary. The airplane began its bucking while we were still close to the ground, as if it might take a leap and nosedive. This solidity and willfulness of the air, a substance I was used to moving through without obstacle, separated us from the ordinary. We traveled east, with the early morning sun ahead, and as we moved over the lakes and rivers and streams they melted and glowed. The landscape was like a map with the water marked out in puddles of smooth golden metal. I was bewitched, of course.

It wasn't the first time I'd been on a plane. I had taken planes to Chicago and back when I went there to college, since flying wasn't much more expensive than taking the train. I went to a Catholic girls' school that was struggling to reconcile Vatican II with the Middle Ages. I was famous in college chiefly for being able to fall asleep anywhere — sometimes, in fact, in the middle of parties — but at least half of the time I was faking, out of boredom and curiosity. In my letters to Len I would tell him what I had overheard men saying about me when they thought I was sleeping.

Carol Ann and Simon and Simon's father, Mr. Carpinisian, met me at La Guardia, and we plunged into traffic in New York. Mr. Carpinisian, a small wizened man wearing a beret, sat on one of the jump seats in the cab. He told me how lousy New York was — too expensive, too crowded, too ugly. I wanted him to stop; I wanted to feel intensely that I was *in* New York City, and to revel in it. He insisted that Simon let him out on West Ninety-fifth Street and said that he would walk back. He said he would go first to Grace's apartment (Grace was Carol Ann's friend from work with whom I was supposed to stay), or that he would walk from Carol Ann's to Grace's through Central Park. I couldn't follow it all. Go, I thought cruelly. Go and let me be in New York.

And there was the city before me, seen through the enormous window of an enormous yellow taxi (there were gypsy cabs as well, in all colors: green, magenta, checked, spotted, two-tone like spectator pumps). There were vans full of balloons, a store window where everything had Mickey Mouse on it. Crowds of people were crossing against the light: shoulders square, chins up, as if they were going to the Crusades. I saw a fruit stand with pumpkins spilling out on the sidewalk; skinny little black boys dancing on corners; phalanxes of grave men in suits wielding briefcases; women in the latest everything. I could barely restrain myself from asking if it was always like this.

The street where Grace lived was like a movie set. Tall, narrow houses stood up against each other, actually touching. There were heavy stone balustrades and iron grilles, lacy and elegant. A vine twined green right up the front of Grace's brownstone. As we got out of our cab, Simon and Carol Ann pointed out the San Remo down the street — towers where famous people slept, smoked cigarettes, made toast.

Grace's apartment wasn't romantic, but it was different from anything I'd ever seen. There was only one window in the front room, and it opened on an airshaft and a fire escape. Back the other way ran a narrow chain of long, dark rooms with high ceilings. In the front room, I sat down on a green chair; Simon and Carol Ann were on the brown couch, with a scarred coffee table in front of them. Grace hovered. Should we go out to dinner? Should we wait for Vito? Should we call Vito? Or would he be annoyed? I didn't know who Vito was. Then the matter of a wedding present from Simon to Carol Ann — should he give it to her now or in the morning? Before or after the ceremony? He went to Grace's kitchen, six feet away, to call his mother, while we pretended not to listen. I had hardly looked at Carol Ann until now.

But it was all too much for me — too much marriedness, happiness. I was there, I guessed, to be widow of honor. I tried to keep from thinking anything while Simon put the wedding pearls around Carol Ann's neck after his mother gave the O.K. They were moony and translucent against her skin. I thought how eccentric it was for me to have brought the Dream Club book with me (it was in my purse that very minute) — how theatrical. Did I think I was in a soap opera? I wanted to ask Carol Ann if she had dreamed Simon. She had waited so long to get married and now she was doing it in such a calm, deliberate way that it seemed that she must have foreknowledge. What else did she know?

But I kept the book hidden, and we all went to a restaurant where there were endless taco chips and frozen margaritas that turned slushy and pleasantly gritty on the tongue. Carol Ann flirted with the waiter while Simon looked on confidently. Grace and I drank a lot. I told stories about things Carol Ann and Kate and I used to do. I found out who Vito was: Grace's ex-lover, whom she still occasionally saw, and who was invited to the wedding for some reason. No one said anything about Len, of course.

The next morning — Saturday, the morning of the wedding — Grace's current lover, Walter, came over to shave in our bathroom while I was still in my robe. Came over from where? I never found out. We drank Bloody Marys while Grace tried to decide whether or not to wear the belt of her dress.

The wedding was in a chapel way over on the East Side. It was just right, mixing hesitation and instinctive correctness; we all came spilling out onto the side street afterward feeling new and virtuous. The reception was in a French restaurant two blocks away, past more New Yorkness: two old men — drunk or asleep, I didn't know which — lying on the sidewalk, with the sun shining down on the street past the sharpness of the buildings, and people hurrying by in leather and glittery plastic.

We walked down four steps into the restaurant, into gray softness pricked by lights like stars set in the ceiling. We ate unidentifiable appetizers — my favorite was pâté on triangles of white bread studded with what seemed to be tiny chocolate flowers. We sat down to beef Wellington, with green beans tied in little bundles by a ring of carrot shaved to a thin curl, and a pale-orange pasta. The cake was lofty and crystalline, with a shell of hard meringue icing. Later on, some people were singing "Norwegian Wood" in the bathroom.

I drank champagne and listened to everyone talking marriage, husbands, wives, divorce, former husbands, former wives, lovers, engagements. It reminded me of what happens at a baby shower, where everyone seems compelled to talk about labor pains and toilet training. Here, there were horror stories of parting, tears, money, lovers, dinners congealed or burned, blows, tiffs over toothpaste and laundry.

"You'll find a good man," Carol Ann's mother told Grace, and Grace nodded, unconvinced.

When I went over to sit with Carol Ann at the bar, I swayed a little, and she swayed on her barstool. "So how long is it since Len died?" she asked.

"Two," I said. "Two years."

"Let's see, that's what — six hundred days?"

"More," I said.

The man sitting next to Carol Ann on the other side got out his pocket calculator and figured it laboriously. "Seven hundred thirty days," he said.

"Thank you, sweetie." Carol Ann turned back to me. "You know the thing about three hundred and sixty-five days a year — I don't believe in them. I don't feel like there can really be that many sometimes."

"Hold still a minute," I said. I leaned over and carefully repinned her roses, which were drooping just below the cloudy pearls.

"So why didn't Kate come, anyway?"

"She figured there wouldn't be any cute guys."

"Did I ever tell you how Grace and I used to use fake Waspy names when we went out and picked guys up in bars?" Carol Ann said. "I was Lindsay and she was Courtney."

I said, "Did I ever tell you I had a fantasy that I got amnesia and went away somewhere on a Greyhound bus and fell in love with a mechanic and had four kids and lived in a trailer?"

This got a big laugh, but the point was, of course, that if I had amnesia when I came to, it would not be my trailer, they would not be my kids, the man with his name written in fancy script over his pocket and with a collection of baseball caps would not be really mine. If I lost them, it would just be like waking up to another world – an occasion for puzzlement instead of sadness.

But death – let's face it, who cares? It's important, sure; everybody will acknowledge this. But, as they say, no one wants to hear about it. If it were something you could wish for, something you might not get, it would be different. Where's the suspense?

And where is all this taking us? To the part about life going on – the man I meet in New York, maybe, or back at home, marriage, everything? After all, why not a baby? A house in the country with a fireplace and a tractor and, yes, a pony. But even if I had all that and more, had the love of this new man and a garden where I managed to grow delphiniums of a completely new color, like angel's eyes, even if I was good as gold for the rest of my life, it would simply make no difference. It's fine to wish for things, but when you get them you still have your life to live somehow.

But there is still my dream in the heart of New York City – the dream I had sleeping in Grace's apartment near the San Remo and just four blocks up from the Dakota, where John Lennon was living: my dream on a sofa bed made up for me personally by Grace, both of us so drunk from the wedding and the after-wedding and the bar after that that we collapsed it twice. After, I lay down in the foreign dark and slept – it was the night before Halloween, the eve of All Hallows Eve – and I remember how I imagined the lost souls winging, flitting, whatever, through the air as thickly as leaves: thin little wrinkled white things as insubstantial as airmail stationery. And this was New York, a whole plane flight away from home, with a strange pillow and blanket. But I slept anyway, and when I woke up I'd had a dream.

I dreamt that I was watching television with Kate, a talk show on which someone announced the results of a poll: What would Americans answer to the question, "Would you go with an alien who invited you to take a ride in his spaceship?"

Thirty-two percent said yes. I said yes, but the yes was for Len, because that's what he would have said if they'd polled him on a street corner, or on the phone (how do they do that anyway?), and I saw him — in the dream, you understand — on television saying yes to an alien, who was thin and green and silver, with long, long fingers and eyes like lava, quick and molten. Len was thinking of me, of course, while he was saying yes, and he was walking up the steps, or ramp, or ladder that led into the spaceship. But when I woke up in New York City I knew perfectly well that he would only have been thinking of what the controls would be like, if they were as good as the latest in special effects, the best technology from the right places, and I knew that not one thought did he give to me, not one. He was thinking ahead about whether he would get to drive it or not.

When I woke up, Grace was making instant coffee, and she began immediately to tell me about Vito, who had never come to the wedding at all, and it came out how he was irresponsible and six years younger than she was.

"Or is it seven?" she said. "But no, it's only six, I guess, because here we are in 1978, and he was born in 1958."

I felt surprise that someone could be twenty years old who had been born seven years after me. Yes, I said to myself, that's how much room there is in the universe, and I felt those tightly packed years shrug and rub a little against each other. But I kept my attention on what Grace was saying about this man I was never going to meet, because it was interesting, and I wanted to tell Kate about it when I got home. I watched Grace's face, listened to her voice rise and fall. I was in New York. It was October. If I wanted, I could go out and have margaritas for breakfast.

TEENAGERS LIVING
IN CLEVELAND

::

1

I'm lying on my bed and talking to Kristin, but what I'm really doing is looking out the window at the O'Brien — it's Mike — who's outside right now. They are so cute, all of them, even Billy, the little one. He's only six or seven, but I imagine that he's what a baby would look like if I had one with Jesse or Jason or Mike after we got married. Claudia O'Brien: I've written it in my notebook about a million times. Mike is working on his car, just fooling around with it like guys do. I really know that Mike's out, I'm not that totally unrealistic. He's nineteen. Way too old.

"Mike's outside my window right this minute," I tell Kristin.

"I could die for Mike," she says.

"You've got a chance of zero percent," I say. "And what about A.J.?"

"My brother says he's bad for me and I should get him out of my system. But he's so cute."

"What does your brother know anyway?" I say. "Does he think he's Dear Abby or what?"

"Did I tell you what happened when he walked by my locker on his way to English?"

I'm holding the phone upside down during this part because I've heard it all before. Outside, Mike closes his car hood and starts picking all his junk up. He's a very neat person. Jason is more of a slob, and fourteen just like me. Jesse is fifteen, exactly one year older than I am, which is the perfect age. Jesse is the O'Brien I like the best but no one in the world knows this.

2

My sister, Vicky, is eating all the Cheerios out of the box along with spoonfuls of grape jelly. This is her new thing to eat after school. I used to eat toast with yogurt when I was her age, which is eleven and a half, but that isn't as totally gross. Now I eat pretzels with milk.

We are both waiting for the phone to ring. She is waiting for one of her dopey friends to call her so they can talk swim-team stuff. I am waiting for Kristin to call me and maybe tell me that we're going to the movies and meet A.J. and some other guy. I don't expect to like this other guy, but it's practice.

"I bet my hair is harder on top than yours," Vicky says to me.

"Don't be such a kid," I say.

When the phone rings we both jump at it, but it's for me.

"It's all set," Kristin says. "We're going to meet them at ten minutes to eight. This other guy drives, A.J. said, and his hair is spiked, not really extreme though."

"What if my mom makes me take Vicky?" I say.

"That's all I need."

"Well, I can't exactly tell her like 'Mom, Kristin and I are like going to meet some boys and so Vicky would be in the way.' "

"God, I can't believe this."

"Well, maybe she won't," I say.

3

I am lying on my bed with my head hanging over the edge. Vicky is on the other bed doing the same. When we were little we had a game we played like this, it was so secret that no one knew about it, not even Mom. We did it at night before we fell asleep. We had secret names. If we asked each other questions in this game we had to answer the truth.

"So what happened when A.J. didn't come?" she says.

"Kristin was really pissed," I say. "Especially when this other guy Louis came." We laugh, which makes your nose feel weird when you're upside down.

"So was he cute?"

"He was O.K. He was somebody from the Bryant playground."

"Who?"

"You know the girl who used to fall down when she made a basket and act really dumb?"

Vicky shakes her head. Her upside-down hair switches back and forth.

"Well, it was her brother."

"Oh."

"So what'd you do?" I say to her.

"I went to a sleepover at Jennifer Reinhardt's house. We had pizza and chips and pop and we watched a movie. Then we wanted to watch MTV but Jennifer made us watch a tape of her sister's wedding that she was in. And then this one girl thought she smelled gas and she said she really knew what it smelled like because her mother blew up the oven once, so Jennifer went and woke her parents up, but it wasn't gas so they yelled at us. Then we did the Ouija board until everybody fell asleep. It said I was going to be a dog trainer and have eight children."

"Remember when we had the dog for three days before we found out Mom was allergic to it?"

"Yeah." Vicky sighs and lifts her legs up, pointing her toes at the ceiling. "Do you want to get out his collar and look at it?"

"No," I say. "Not tonight."

4

We are walking across the parking lot behind Sears, Kristin and me, over to where the Pick-n-Pay used to be. Kristin points to a sign that says INTERNATIONAL MARKETERIA — "That's it," she says.

I am feeling nervous about going in. It still looks like a Pick-

n-Pay except that the words are gone. You can see the places
where they were, but they're not there anymore. There are
lots of little tables with dirty old junk on them and people
standing around picking it up and looking at it like it was
diamonds — old mixing bowls, TV antennas with no TV,
shoes that have been worn by somebody. I start to hang back
a little.

"Are you sure this is the right place?" I say to Kristin. We
stop.

"Sure I'm sure." We both look through the doors, which
still look just like a supermarket's doors, the kind that open
automatically. We can't see inside because the doors are dirty
and have papers and cards stuck all over them.

"Well, do you want to go in?" I say. I open my purse
and take out the strawberry kissing gel I just bought at the
drugstore.

"Sure, don't you?"

"Sure," I say. I'm thinking it might be better inside, or that
when we get in it will turn out that you need a card or a
membership or something and we'll have to leave. "So let's
go."

"Let me borrow that a minute first," Kristin says, and
I give her the kissing gel and watch her smooth it on her
lips with her little finger. It's a different color on her than
on me.

The doors don't open by themselves anymore so we have
to push them, but when we get inside it is O.K. There is
nobody to stare at us like we don't belong or ask us for
anything, just a lot of people looking at stuff and not paying
attention to us. It is like a flea market, except not outside —

rows and rows of tables with people sitting behind them and other people moving up and down from one table to the next. The first table has all kinds of tapes and the guy sitting behind it has a beard and a turban. The next is shelves of glass animals, all sizes, and then one for T-shirts where you can have anything printed on that you want.

Kristin and I stop at a booth with only earrings and start holding them up next to our ears. "These are really cheap," I say. "You know, this would be a really great place to go Christmas shopping."

Kristin is looking around.

"Did you hear me, batbrain?" I say to her.

"Do you see anything that looks like fortune-telling?" she asks.

I turn in a circle and look. "No."

"Come on, we'll have to walk around."

"Couldn't we ask someone?" I say, because the earring lady looks pretty nice. She is smoking a cigarette and talking to the glass-animal lady at the next table. But Kristin has already moved on and I follow her.

Mostly the people at the tables don't say anything when you walk by unless you happen to look them in the eyes, so I'm careful to look at everything around them. One man says something anyway, "Hey, you two, hey honey," he is saying but I ignore him and walk faster. We keep going up and down the aisles — there is so much stuff — and after a while I start to think that the girl at school was wrong about the place or that the fortune-teller has left, and really, I'm pretty happy about that.

But then Kristin grabs my arm and shakes it. "There she is," she says. "There she is over there."

She's in the next row. We passed her from behind already and didn't notice because there is nothing special about her space except that she doesn't have anything in it to sell. There are just a lot of metal folding chairs, making a square around her where she sits at an old card table with another chair across from her, empty.

"Come on," Kristin says, and I say "Wait," at the same time, because I don't like the way the woman looks. She looks very ordinary. Her clothes are not too cool, but ordinary for a woman as old as her, a pink sweater that is too tight over her stomach and a plain skirt. Her face is ordinary, sort of fat, and she is smoking. I don't like it that she is smiling all the time.

"I'll kill you if you won't go over with me," Kristin says.

"All right, all right," I say.

When we come up to her she turns her head all of a sudden and looks at us, still smiling. "You girls want your fortune told?" she says, with her smile staying on her face the whole time.

"Yeah," Kristin says.

"Five dollars each," she says, and puts out her cigarette. "Cards or crystal?"

Kristin and I count our money over again although we already know how much there is: seven dollars and eighty-three cents. "We can only get one," Kristin says.

"That's O.K.," I say. "You're the one who needs to know something."

"For seven-fifty, I do two short readings," the woman says, and she lights another cigarette.

"No," I say, because if we spend that much we won't have enough money for McDonald's.

"I'll tell you what," she says, leaning toward me and smiling even harder, "for a dollar extra I'll answer one question for the second seeker."

"O.K." Kristin says. I shrug my shoulders. Kristin gives her the money and sits in the chair across from her. I start to sit in one of the other chairs, but the woman puts up her hand and says no, that I can't listen. So I go back over to the earring table and watch from there how the woman lays out her cards in front of Kristin. A steady stream of smoke goes up from her cigarette. Once she puts her hand on Kristin's hand and my own hand twitches.

When Kristin gets up, she waves for me to come over, but I shake my head no. Kristin comes over and pushes me. "Come on," she says. "We paid for it. Don't be mental."

I go over and sit down. The woman looks at me. "One question," she says. "For this, the crystal, not the cards. Think hard to make it a good one." She has the crystal on the table in front of her, a ball of glass in a holder that is just ordinary plastic. When you look into the ball you can see colors and shapes moving but this is just from what's outside it.

"Come on, what'll it be?" she says to me, but I can't think how to ask anything I want to know.

"Never mind," she says. "I know what you want. There is a boy. You want to know about this boy, right?"

I nod yes, but I am not impressed, because this is probably what everyone wants to know.

"Well, I will tell you." She cups her hands over the ball, fingers not touching, and then springs them apart. "You will get what you want, but you cannot wait for it to happen. You must take the initiative. You must make the first move and step into your future." She smiles at me even harder, and waves for me to go. "Right?" she says.

5

I am writing a secret letter to Jesse. This is not a letter to send, no matter what the fortune-teller said. But I am imagining sending it while I write. I imagine how things would be between us if I could send it.

Dear Jesse — no — *My Dearest Jesse* — or no, maybe something more bizarre? Or maybe just very intense, only his first name — *Jesse,*

When I saw you in history today I had a weird feeling in my stomach — but no, I don't want to talk about my stomach, that's too gross — *I had this weird feeling like you were going to talk to me* — or maybe what I should say is that I had a dream about him. This is what Kristin says she always says and it works great — *I suddenly remembered that I had this dream about you, that you and I were in the gym* — although actually we were in the girls' locker room, but I can't say that — *and you put your hand on my shoulder and told me you liked my sweater, that it looked so cool with my hair.* — But what would I say after that?

In the dream in the girls' locker room he put his hand on my shoulder and told me he could never love me like I wanted because he was leaving immediately to go to Washington where he was going to live the rest of his life with a team that played basketball for the president, and then the floor started to slide away, just wash away like a picture that gets wet, and he stood there shaking my hand until I slid away with the floor, holding on to his hand until it turned to water. Kristin could maybe do something with this.

But it doesn't make any difference, because I'm not going to send it anyway, right? —

Jesse,

Last night I dreamed about you and we were so close in this dream that I could hardly breathe — that's good — *so close that I could see into your mind. We belong together, it's fate. I will be everything to you. Years from now you'll look at me tenderly and say thanks. When we go to prom together in two years everybody will say we are the perfect couple.* — This is dumb. What could I really say?

I hear my sister outside thumping something against the garage, my mother washing the dishes with the radio turned up high; my father is down in the basement doing something with tools, I know, but I can't hear him. The O'Briens are quiet next door, invisible in their house. There is a basketball on their driveway, moving a little one way and a little the other way when the wind blows —

Jesse,

What did we have for homework in history on Monday? I was talking to Kristin, you know, that girl with curly hair — no, don't mention Kristin, dummy — *I was talking to somebody and didn't hear what pages to read. Don't you hate it when they don't write it on the board? Write the page numbers on this paper.*

Claudia

P.S. I saw you in the game last week and you were really good.

I could send this, I think. Maybe not the P.S. But maybe it's O.K. It's probably O.K. if I say "pretty good."

6

We are at Grandma's for dinner, us and Markie, our aunt, and her boyfriend, and the little cousins that are Mom and Aunt Markie's cousin Carol Ann's kids. The kids and Vicky and me are fighting about who is going to sit where. I'm going along with it, but I don't really feel like it. It's dinner, isn't it? and it only lasts for a half hour, so who cares? I used to always want the seat by Aunt Markie but I let little Julie get it without even fighting for it.

"Now you kids," Grandma says, bringing in more dishes of things to eat.

"Bernadette, sit down and eat," Grandpa says.

"I've just got to wait in here and get this coffee perking," she says back.

"No eating until your grandmother sits down," Mom says, and we all pretend we don't have anything in our mouths.

"Go ahead and start, go ahead," Grandma says from the kitchen.

"We're just putting food on our plates, Mother, we're not eating a thing until you get in here," Mom says. She puts green beans on Julie's plate.

Aunt Markie passes the rolls to Dad. Dad passes the gravy to me. I pass it to Grandpa without taking any.

"What, are you on a diet, Miss Skinny?" he says.

"Here I am, I'm sitting down," Grandma says. "Pass me the salad."

"I need a spoon," one of the little kids says.

"I'll get it," Grandma says, starting to get up and everybody yells at her at the same time to sit down and they will get it.

"All right, all right," Grandma says and everybody laughs. Vicky and I look at each other and raise our eyebrows.

"Has everybody got potatoes?" Grandma says. "Has Grandpa got some? What about Julie, she hasn't got any." She looks closer at Julie. "Why is Julie crying?"

Julie's mom gets up and goes over to her.

"Don't be a baby," her brother says.

"But what's wrong, honey?" her mom says. "I can't fix it if you don't tell me."

Julie whispers in her mom's ear.

"What did she say?" Grandma says.

"It's the beans," Julie's mom says. "She doesn't like the beans."

"But why doesn't she like the beans?" Grandma says. "They're so good, Julie. Try one for Grandma."

Julie yells that she hates beans, that they're a yucky color.

"Your dress is the same color on the pocket as those beans," her brother says.

Julie tries to hit him. Her mom takes her away to the back bedroom. All the grown-ups smile and laugh a little. Even Vicky smiles. Grandma is smiling when she takes Julie's plate into the kitchen to keep it warm.

I can't stand this, I think. I can't stand to be here. I'd like to be in the back bedroom with Julie telling her she was right to cry. Or I should be out in the dark somewhere with my friends when we walk down the street in the night, when we are outside in the dark and there are the shut doors and the people shut away inside with the light, when we laugh and talk loud and play our radios to push the dark hard up against the light inside.

"We have apple cobbler for dessert," Grandma says.

"Claudia, you and Vicky get the plates and the spoons. I'll cut and you can pass around."

7

This is chemistry. Jesse is not in this class with me, he is only in my history class. But Kristin sits right next to me. Mr. Flashman is putting formulas for something on the board but no one is watching. No one ever listens to what he says except when it is lab, so nothing gets blown up or anything. In the back two guys are flooding one of the sinks and doing Viking funerals. They have these paper boats they made and they set them on fire. This class is pretty wild. A guy stuck the rubber-handled tongs in the wall socket once and shorted out this whole part of the school. One time they put these little beakers upside down under the four legs of Mr. Flashman's chair so they broke when he sat down. He got really mad that time.

"So what's going on with A.J.," I say to Kristin.

"You've got to call him up tonight and ask him something for me," she says.

"Why can't you call him?"

"It'll be better if you do."

"You're weird."

"So, will you?"

"What do I have to ask him?"

"I'll write it out for you."

"Is this about his old girlfriend?"

"You have to call before eight or his mother won't let him talk on the phone."

I watch the two boys in the back fooling around with these little bottles of chemicals left over from like 1910 that are in the backs of all the drawers. They pour a bottle of some clear stuff into one of the big beakers with some other clear stuff in it and it turns blue.

"This is going to be on the test, class," Mr. Flashman says.

8

Vicky and I are raking leaves on the part of the lawn next to the O'Briens' house. I can see their mother inside doing something in the kitchen and I can hear one of them playing the radio on the station I like best.

"What'd you do in school?" I ask her.

"This girl I know was telling us stuff about Cher. She said she went to visit her in Hollywood when they went to California on vacation."

"You didn't believe her, did you?"

"She said Cher showed her all her tattoos. She had one on her left foot, one on her right shoulder, one on her arm, and two in unmentionable places. That means her butt, probably, don't you think?"

"She read it in a magazine."

"Well, that's what I thought. She said Cher lent her a nightgown when she stayed overnight."

"Listen, Vicky. I've got to use the phone for a while after supper," I say. "So talk to Mom or something so she doesn't come and tell me to get off."

"Why should I?"

"Don't be a dweeb."

"I bet you're going to call a boy."

"Shut up," I say.

"You're going to call Jesse, I bet, aren't you?"

"Shut up," I say, and I'm glad she's nowhere near right.

9

After supper, I get out the questions. I know I'm going to feel really stupid doing this. I read the list over:

1. Was he at the game with his old girlfriend?
2. If he was, did he ask her to go ahead of time?
3. Did he, on the way out, hold her hand or not? If he did, then why did he?
4. Does he still like her? As a friend or a girlfriend?
5. Did he ever like Kristin or was he just using her?
6. If he says he likes Kristin, then ask him if he's going to the social on Friday.

Really stupid. I am dialing the phone anyway. A.J.'s mother answers and I have to tell her who I am before she will get him on the phone. She says to say hello to my mother for her. Then there's a long wait, like he's in the bathroom or something.

"Hello?" he says.

"Hi," I say. "This is Claudia."

"I know," he says.

"I have to ask you some stuff. For Kristin."

"Oh-oh," he says.

"Come on," I say, "just let me ask you. It'll only take a minute."

"How're you going to know if I'm telling the truth?"

Who cares, I'm thinking. "I'll know," I say, real seriously — stern, like a teacher.

"O.K. I can take it."

So I ask him. And he says just what I expected. How he met his old girlfriend there by accident, and sure, he still has feelings for her, but he really likes Kristin, but he just doesn't know yet whether she's more a friend or a girlfriend to him. And he's coming to the social.

"Are you coming?" he says to me.

"Who wants to know?"

"Louis does." Then there's this noise like fighting and he drops the phone. I wait. Louis is the guy who came to the movies, who used to go to Bryant playground.

"Louis wants to talk to you," he says.

"It's O.K. with me," I say.

"Hello, is this Claudia?"

"Uh-huh," I say.

"Listen, do you want to go for a walk?"

10

"You want to go down and look at Bryant?" he said.

"Sure," I said.

I even told Mom where I was going, because this is so unserious. When we walked by the O'Briens' house I thought how Jesse might be looking out the window and see me with this other boy. But if he didn't, that's O.K., I guess. We

walked down to the playground, and then we sat on the
swings for a while, and talked about how far along he was in
math compared to me, and then we sat on the jungle gym
and he hung upside down for a while and then we walked
home. For all I know, I might never see him again.

Sitting on the porch now with Louis, I can feel Vicky
crouched down hiding at the side of the house, looking at me
through the railing. She is spying on Louis and me to see if
we kiss or something, I guess. She knows I know she's there.
Louis was telling me about how he's going to play in the new
league this summer, and how he and A.J. want to get an old
car they can fix up together, even though they can't drive it
yet — A.J. lied about his driving. But now he has stopped
talking, he is rubbing his one finger over and over a rough
place on the floor of the porch. I can hear Vicky sniffling, but
I'm not even mad at her, I'm too busy feeling how I am really
in my body. I like the feel of my feet in my socks, the curve
of my hand on my chin. I like the way the house across the
street looks with its fat clipped bushes. I like the tree in front
of our house that is like a cave of leaves, the little wind
moving the leaves and my hair, and the blue sky.

STEALING TIME

::

Let's not go, I say, even though I do not really mean this. Kate says that she was in a good mood all morning, but the closer she got to my house — no offense — the more depressed she got. We say, what's new? I tell Kate about the night before at the bar — Jay and Allie, blah, blah, Jim and Lynette, blah, blah, how Jim said the kids broke the bed. Kate tells me how Claudia wrote her birthday list in purple crayon.

We go to the bathroom together — an old habit. I comb my hair, looking over her shoulder while she puts on lipstick. Let's go before we lose our nerve, we say — we'll go and get it over with and we won't have to go again for a long time. I put on my scarf, she puts on her gloves, and we go out to the car. You drive, she says. No, you, I say, and she does.

As she starts the car, I move the foil-wrapped pot of begonias out of the way. Pink, damp, they scent the car. She says what else then? and I tell her about the fight at the bar last night. There were four women sitting at the table two tables over from where I was sitting with Jim and Lynette, and one of them was fat, and one was fat and ugly, and one was fat, ugly, and mean. And the fourth? Kate asks. The fourth was average-looking — not fat, not mean. And I tell her how I had noticed them before the fight because they talked loud and because they went out on forays into the bar, looking for someone to dance with or to buy them a drink, and then coming back in between songs or drinks to compare notes. One of them said, "I had to ask three guys before I found a son of a bitch who was game." Her name was Marcella and she was the one who got into the fight just before the bar closed. She accused someone at another table of looking at her in a certain unpleasing way; the looker accused Marcella of dropping cigarette ash in her drink; then they fought and then Marcella accused her of breaking her glasses. The police were called because the bouncer (who was really the bar owner's mother-in-law) felt unequal to the task. When we left, there were two police cars and fifteen or twenty people in the parking lot, but no action. "She started it, let her finish it," Marcella was saying to one of the policemen.

It's a dumb story, but we laugh hard enough to make our stomachs hurt, and that takes us all the way to the hospital.

Parking. The pedestrian ramp has a sign that says PEDESTRI-ANS ONLY, NO VEHICLES and we discuss the possibility of a chase scene and the problem posed for vehicles by the steps, the difficulties of turning a car to the right or the left at the bottom, where the steps give way to a narrow driveway. It can't be done, we decide. At the hospital desk, we ask for Aunt Ren. The receptionist wears perfect fuchsia lipstick that just misses the points of her upper lip; it's laid on thick, with a chiseled edge, vivid purple against brown. She gives us cards and complicated directions: south, D-Ward, North Corridor, desk on left. Did you get that? Kate says. No, I say.

We watch ourselves in a mirror wall while we wait for the elevator. We see with relief that we look good — no older, our hair is O.K. Upstairs, there is a twisting way through doors and corridors to the A-Wing and a big open room that looks out over the city. We are here.

Our cousin, Graham, is sitting there with Aunt Ren, his mother. She is blue and white — blue dress, white hair, pale skin. He is golden — tan, blondish hair, gold-and-white shirt, tan slacks, gold watch. She cries when we come in. She cries when Kate opens up the pot of begonias. It's the stroke, Graham says. We know. We talk: about his house; his wife, Laura; his son's wedding; how Laura must buy a dress. Laura will come tomorrow. Laura understands Aunt Ren better than he does, he says. It is like charades. Graham has things to say about kids today, real estate, American cars. He says how his daughter wants a phone, a car, to move out. I say my twenty-year high-school reunion will be this year, ha ha. I did not get to my tenth because I was in a bad mood.

Graham occasionally talks as if Aunt Ren is not there, but it is hard not to. She tries to tell us about something that looks like climbing. A rope? A ladder? She does this several times and is frustrated when we don't know what she means. Graham takes his opportunity and leaves. We say what a handsome son he is, and she looks over her shoulder with difficulty to watch him all the way out the door.

She makes it plain somehow that she wants to go back to her room; she walks with difficulty, leaning on our arms. She knows where her room is. Her roommate, Stella, is there, lying in bed, younger and more alert than Aunt Ren. The TV is on, showing a pro bowling tournament; the room is full of sun. We help Aunt Ren into the wheelchair. She is heavy, hard to move. I look out the window. We're on the eighth floor, and you can see out across the city. I say that you should be able to see Blessed Sacrament from here but you can't. Blessed Sacrament, I explain to Stella — our old parish.

Leaning against the hospital-room windowsill in the sun, we eat chocolate eggs, foil-wrapped, purple, pink, gold. Aunt Ren says something to Stella, who understands her, although we cannot. Stella answers that the nurse didn't come, that she herself has been in bed since two o'clock, and that her arm is caught underneath her.

"Is it still?" I ask. "Maybe I could fix it." And I do, I pull it out.

"It's paralyzed," Stella says.

"Where shall I put it?" I say.

She asks me to put it on her chest, crossed with the other arm. "Here," she says, "where I can keep ahold of it."

Kate makes a place for the begonias among the dozen or so other plants and flower arrangements. I read the cards to Aunt Ren that are taped up on the wall. I read out the hospital-activities calendar — movies, bingo, a magician. (Aunt Ren wrinkles her face to express distaste, and I have a sudden picture of a young man, skinny in a sweatshirt, doing tricks with ties and balloons and bunches of cloth flowers for a group of old people in wheelchairs, in bathrobes and slippers.) I look at her chart and feel bad when I see the part about bladder and bowel control, even though all the marks are positive. I see the announcements on the wall about therapy. I guess then what she was talking about before, with the in-and-out motions of her hands: occupational therapy, baskets, clay. There is a card on the wall that says "Restraint in wheelchair." We say we must leave.

"Why, why?" Aunt Ren says at once.

"Here are the words she can say," Stella tells us now, suddenly chatty. "She can say 'nothing,' 'oh, my God,' 'yes,' 'no,' 'what,' 'why,' 'same.' "

"Nothing," Aunt Ren says after Stella. "Nothing, nothing."

When we leave, we hear them talking together. She wants to tell Stella, is telling her somehow, that we are her nieces, Markie and Kate, the daughters of her sister Bernadette. That we used to live upstairs from her long ago, that she looked after me when my mother was in the hospital delivering my sister, that she braided my hair, and that I had Cheerios for breakfast.

On the way out, we see no nurse or attendant. The desk is deserted. I think how we could go and look at the records, read the patients' mail, steal the microscopes, the centrifuge, whatever — all left in unlocked, doors-open rooms. In the hospital, the sun is everywhere, shining through the modern sheets of glass onto the red, blue, or orange vinyl seats of the modern stackable chairs; in one of the waiting rooms, a nurse, the only one we have seen, leans against the glass looking at the city. By the elevator there is a canvas laundry receptacle filled with sheets; we imagine blood.

Not so bad, we say on the way out. The electronic box that is supposed to show our parking fee shows only the broken outlines of the numbers; we take on faith the attendant's announcement that we owe seventy cents. We wait at the traffic light. "Let's go see Blessed Sacrament," I say.

"You only say that because I'm driving," Kate says. But she gets into the right lane and we drive down Trowbridge. Children playing in the street scatter in front of us. We come to the crossing where we used to turn onto Trowbridge from Thirty-fifth — where the crossing guard, an older boy, once threatened to report me to the principal because I crossed not at the corner.

"It's so narrow," Kate says.

"We were little," I say.

The church, the parking lot that was the boys' playground, the nuns' house, the priest's house, where I went only twice — once when I was sick, once to see Monsignor Ryan lying dead, in state. I ask Kate if she saw that, too.

"Yes," Kate says. "Mother took me to see him. Can you believe she did that?"

"Yes," I say, although I don't know why.

We turn a corner and here we are at Carol Makowski's store, where we were not allowed to go; my friend DeeDee's house. Left on Fulton: Grandma's house, the fire station.

"Sometimes I hated to go to Grandma's house for lunch," Kate says.

"I still dream about Grandma's backyard," I say. And now I remember the trees, and the gate to the alley, and the stained-glass window at the top of the stairs. We loved the alley because it was brick, empty — secret, like a hidden path. We used to go down it from Grandma's to Aunt Ren's; down to movies at the Lyceum; down to the Dairy Dell, with its green, cool, marble soda fountain; down to our old street, our old house, which looks the same, except it is blue.

There is a car in the driveway. We park in front, pointed the wrong way. "How did they ever move away?" Kate says, meaning our parents. I say that was their generation's thing — to move away, to move up, out. "Ours is different," I say, but I am not sure; I am trying this on Kate.

She looks gloomy. I tell her how Mother told the grandchildren stories about our old neighbor, Anna Jarosz, whose house — former house — we are facing. How her husband broke a garage windowpane by accident and when he was upset she said, "What is it — a window? It's nothing. Watch," and she broke all the other panes in the window: bing, bing, bing. How she made her first husband give her the money to come back to America when he tricked her into going to Yugoslavia to live. "It was so primitive, you wouldn't believe it if I tell you — water from a well in the middle of the village, and what they did to make sure the girls were pure — " Here she would lower her voice so that all I could hear was "a bloody sheet . . ."

Kate starts the car. "I'm going to the mall," she says.

Are we going to Mother's on Sunday?

Will we have lunch with Lynette or will we make an excuse?

The kids are of course impossible.

When we get to my street there is a police car on the corner, and as we drive around it we see a group of people looking at a car that is trapped inside the green chain-link fence around the yard of the corner house. The car, which is pointed out toward the street, has smashed head-on into the telephone pole on the corner. It is impossible at first to see how this might have happened, although the torn-up sod shows where it drove across the lawn and petals from a torn rosebush litter the exposed earth. It is as if the car had simply materialized — a crushing force from some other dimension. The car is a big-finned, shiny-chrome fifties job. As we drive up to my house, my husband, Len, comes walking toward us, and all up and down the street people are standing on their porches or coming down their front walks or peering from behind their screen doors, with their arms hugged across their chests.

"I'm sorry we're late," I say.

"Did that just happen?" Kate says, pointing at the corner.

"I don't know," he says. "I was just tired of staying inside. I wanted to see the sun."

BUYING A PUMPKIN

::

The pumpkin had rotted in the garage, sunk in on itself, actually seemed to be disappearing into the floor like the wicked witch. His kids yelled and danced around like wild animals while Slater picked it up with the snow shovel and carried it dripping and drooling to the trash, but were serious and full of blame when they got tired of throwing rocks at it.

"You got to buy another one," Jilly said. Mickey and Veronica agreed that this was the way.

"You shoulda got it at the market," Mickey said. "You shoulda kept it on the porch." Mickey was second oldest, pushing for promotion.

Slater felt the heat of his failure; he was not up on pumpkins, and it was especially bad that he got the damn thing at Drug Mart, something he knew Kendra, his wife who had so thoroughly left him, would never have done.

He was losing control. Each night, he rode slower and slower on the way home from the plant to get mentally ready for what he would find. Mickey had his best ideas while Slater was at work. Three days before Halloween, between school

and six o'clock, Mickey had corralled his sister and some kids
from down the street to make a cemetery in the front yard.
It was mostly crosses because nailing two pieces of wood
together was something Mickey knew how to do, but also
two nice cardboard tombstones, raggedly rounded off with
Kendra's sewing scissors, and what Mickey called a monu-
ment — Kendra's marble breadboard that was handed down
from her grandma. The names of dead dogs and fish were
neatly written on attached file cards.

"Whoa," he said. "Jilly must have wrote these, they look
so nice and neat."

"We can leave them up, can't we, Dad?" Jilly asked him.
He looked at her.

"Mom might like to see them when she comes back from
visiting Grandma and Auntie Sis." They all watched him to
see what he would say.

"She might," he said. "Let's take a look here." He took
his time looking, stooping to read each card. " 'Mary Jo and
Baby, R I P,' " he read.

"I found that in a book," Mickey said. "It means 'Rest in
Peace.' "

"Well, I know that. Mary Jo and Baby were looking fine
the last time I saw them."

"Aw, Dad, they been dead a week."

He hadn't noticed, that was a fact. If anyone had asked
him how were Mary Jo and Baby, he would have said fine,
picturing them swimming round and round their bowl, happy
as larks. Who had flushed them? he wondered. Or were they
actually buried here, under his feet? He moved on, feeling
unhappy. Nor did he know what to say about the whole
concept of the cemetery. He decided to admire, to be im-

pressed. He helped to think of gloomy inscriptions, which Jilly carefully printed out. But it made him feel a little creepy, and he sort of missed Mary Jo and Baby, now that he knew they were gone. Mary Jo was named after Jilly's best friend, and Baby was Baby, Kendra had explained to him, because he was smaller. When Slater pointed out that Baby was actually a little bigger, she had said it didn't matter, he was still a little fish. One of his favorite things about Kendra was how she called things "little" — a little bird, a little drink. He'd always liked that in her, but he couldn't say why.

The pumpkin weighed on his mind all that Friday night at the bar. When he'd been getting ready to go like he'd been doing for years on every Friday night since at least when Mickey was born — slicking back his hair, finding his softball jacket that said "Brownie's Bombers" on the back, checking his wallet — he found that all three of them were sitting on the couch not watching TV, looking at him. Kendra wasn't here, he realized. That was what they were silently telling him with their not-watching-TV faces. But how old were they now? Jilly ten, Mickey eight. Veronica was pretty small.

He resumed his hair-combing casually. "You kids be good now for the sitter," he said.

"What sitter?" Mickey wanted to know.

"Why, Helen, of course, your Aunt Helen. You like your Aunt Helen to sit for you, don't you?"

"I don't need a sitter," said Mickey.

"Shut up, Mickey," Jilly said, and they all three turned their heads in the TV direction. Sitting down, they *all* looked small.

Helen said she'd come over, but she had a lot of questions. Had he called Kendra? Had Kendra called him? Had he given

Mickey and Jilly money for their school pictures? And when
she got there she had more to say before she'd even taken off
her coat, all cleverly addressed to the kids. What did they
have for dinner? Oh, pizza, how nice, and Burger King the
night before. She bet they missed their mom. Didn't they
miss their mom?

"Helen," Slater said.

"Oh, Slater, Slater," she said, clutching her coat around
her neck, "I'm not laying any blame, I've got you in my
prayers. Maybe you'd like to talk about it some."

"Helen —"

"To Eugene, if you'd rather. You could give him a call this
minute, he's sanding his spark plugs, you could go right over
to the house."

"Helen, I got to go to Brownie's." Putting on his jacket,
freshly washed by Kendra just before she left for West Virginia, he felt now as if he *must* go. He had said he was going
and he was going to go. "I'm on the darts team."

....

After darts, he bought a shot for Brownie, and then Brownie
bought one for him. "You know where to buy a good pumpkin, Brownie?" he asked.

Brownie set a beer in front of Slater. "Supermarket?"

"Not to eat. One for the kids."

"Nope."

"I got one at Drug Mart but it rotted."

"Kendra still visiting her folks?"

Slater nodded. Brownie shook his head, and wiped the bar
with his apron, something he did to express concern.

"You call her?"

"Nah." Slater had thought of calling, sure, had even got so far as holding the receiver in his hand, fingers ready to dial, but every time he started to think what he would say and what she would say and what he would say back and what she would say back to that. From all this he got either angry or depressed, too full of either emotion to be able to deal with Kendra's voice on the phone, or worse, the cigarette voice that was her great-aunt's.

Brownie wiped Slater's beer bottle and set it back down. He shook his head and went over to the other side of the bar to pour some shots of peach schnapps.

And so Slater didn't feel the way he usually did going home on Friday nights, a little high and glad to be going home, counting off things he wanted to tell Kendra. Sometimes she went out as well, with her friend Melody, and sometimes they would meet at the front door coming home together at the same instant and kiss under the porchlight before who-ever was babysitting, prissy Helen or little girls from the neighborhood, could come and catch them at it. Not tonight though.

Tonight, two nights before Halloween and a week plus two days after Kendra had left because she said he was a pig-headed, irresponsible, rotten she-didn't-know-what, he hurt his foot from stepping on the marble breadboard and stopped for a minute to get the full effect of the cemetery. The lousy three beers he'd had were lying heavy on him and he was unable to come up with any whole feelings or plans. Should he call Kendra or not? Did he want to say he was sorry? Was he? What would he be sorry for? Would the kids bring home school pictures even though he hadn't remembered the

money? Where would he find a pumpkin? Maybe the kids
had forgotten? But he knew in his heart that they had not.

He could see Helen staring at him through the front-door
glass. He would go tomorrow, Saturday, and buy a pumpkin
with the kids — a family thing. He walked firmly up the steps,
swallowing his pride as Helen opened the door.

"Helen, where's a good place to get a damn pumpkin?" he
said.

....

Next morning, when he woke up, the sun streamed across
the bed. The curtains that Kendra had opened each morning
and closed each night were open. They had stayed open for
nine days. Kendra would be mad if she knew he never bothered to shut them, mad if she knew he was using the bed-
spread for a blanket. Each night, she took it off and laid it
over her grandma's rocker that sometimes felt to Slater like
her grandma sitting there in their bedroom. Each morning
she put it back on the bed, smoothing over the disturbances
of the night. This was one of the things Slater twitted her
about if he thought of it. Why make the bed? he would say,
we'll just be messing it up tonight anyway. Kendra tended to
twitch when he said things like this, things that she thought
were improper. When she said "improper" he could hear
Catholic school in her voice. Improper thoughts, for instance;
it always meant sex.

He could hear the cartoon voices on TV, and Mickey's
voice, too, and Veronica crying. "What're you kids doing out
there?" he shouted, to be heard over the TV. No sound from
Mickey and Veronica, while the TV voices went on. He

waited. Jilly appeared in the doorway — so tall, he thought. He had expected her head to be somewhere around the door-knob.

"So what is it?" he said to her.

"You want some breakfast, Daddy?" she said, looking him earnestly in the eye.

"What was all the ruckus?" Trying to get around him already, he marveled. At her age.

"Mickey said he was sorry to Veronica."

"I just thought she should have the facts," said Mickey's invisible voice from behind Jilly. Veronica started crying again, and Jilly disappeared. "Ssh, ssh, you can't ask Daddy," he heard her say, and he groaned, closing his eyes to the sun.

"So do you think you'd like Grape-Nuts, Dad?" asked Mickey, still invisible.

Slater gathered himself together, sat up to look at the day vertically and straight on. "How about an Egg McMuffin, you guys? How about McDonald's?"

It was nippy but bright outside. Everything had a hard edge against the blue, blue sky. His hands were cold on the steering wheel, but since he felt guilty for not having known where Veronica's mittens were when they left the house, he left his own gloves in his jacket pocket. Once out, he felt as if things were happening, good things, perhaps. He could see the pumpkin hanging in the day ahead of them like the full moon.

At McDonald's it was too late for breakfast. But Slater smiled, restraining Mickey's fury at being denied pancakes. He delegated tasks: Mickey to pay, Jilly to carry the tray, Veronica to bring napkins and straws. He would pick their table and wait for them to join him. Everyone was to have a

large order of fries. No dessert. Kendra had very strong opin-
ions about sugar, knowing now what she wished she had
known before spending a decade at the dentist.

Musing, he looked out through the sheet of plate glass at
the brightness of the day. People in cars driving by on errands
unknown to him, children on bikes and skateboards, dogs
ambling and sniffing, airplanes crossing overhead — all this
purpose oppressed him, but he struggled to hold on to his
feeling of resolve. He pulled his notebook from his pocket to
make a list of what was waiting: Pumpkin, he wrote. Get gas.
What was today? The 29th. Halloween was Monday. My
God, what about costumes? And he would have to take them
out on Monday, surely. Costumes? he wrote. Who would
hand out candy? Did they have candy? Grocery store, he
wrote. Probably he would have to buy some other stuff as
well. There had been no bacon when he looked yesterday
and Jilly had pointed out to him that there was only one roll
of toilet paper.

"What're you writing, Dad?" Mickey pushed the tray to
the middle of the table and sat down next to him.

"It's Veronica's turn to sit next to Daddy," Jilly said, bear-
ing another tray.

"She doesn't care," Mickey said, settling firmly in his seat.

"Mickey!" Jilly did something with her voice. What was
it? Slater wondered. She didn't raise it. Was it something that
all women knew, or had she learned it from Kendra? Oh, she
had a voice, Kendra did, even if she couldn't sing. She used
it like an instrument, Slater thought gloomily, to say "I'm
disappointed in you," "What do you think you're doing?,"
"You'd better stop that right now," "You're wonderful," "I

love you" — and all this in just the way she could say your name. He thought of the way she would say his name at certain times, hissing the *s* a little, letting her tongue slide over the *l* and the long sound of the *a*, the *t* hardly there at all before the quick pull up of the last short syllable.

Jilly had inherited this talent, or learned it, for sure: Mickey was changing places with Veronica, though he was making some ferocious faces at nobody in particular.

"Well, kids," Slater started to say, and then got a look at what was on the trays that Jilly was handing around. "What's this?"

All three kids looked at him with that innocent blank look that made him crazy. "What, Daddy?" Veronica said.

"These ice-cream things — what are these?" He felt a pressure in his head. He had no authority, couldn't even make a point with his own children.

"They're sundaes," Mickey said.

"I *know* they're sundaes, I know that. What I want to know is what they're doing here on our table. Didn't I say no desserts?"

"But Daddy — " Jilly began.

"No buts. No buts at all. Back they go. You, Jilly, you take them back."

Immediately Veronica started to cry. Mickey began to attack the underside of the table with murderous kicks, taking advantage of his cowboy boots. Jilly stood and gathered the sundaes, her lip trembling. She picked up the tray and looked him straight in the eye. "It's not fair," she said, and walked away.

"Well," Slater said, but Mickey and Veronica would not

look at him. He drummed his fingers on the table. He opened up his hamburger and took a large bite. "Delicious," he said, watching them out of the corner of his eye. "Nice and hot." Veronica poked at the top of her Happy Meal box, but Mickey folded his arms and looked out the window.

Jilly and the tray returned. Slater saw that she had brought the sundaes back. Had the woman at the counter refused — or had things gotten so bad, he thought, that even Jilly would defy him? He had been depending on Jilly, he realized.

She put the tray down on the table, but didn't say anything. "Jilly," Slater said, trying to put some power in his voice that would convey to her his disappointment and desperation.

"Oh, Slater." He turned to see Kendra's friend Melody coming down the aisle toward them. Shit, double fucking shit, he thought, for he had forgotten that Melody worked at this McDonald's.

"Melody," he said.

"It's all right about the sundaes," Melody said, hanging over him in a sort of feminine crouch. He could smell her perfume and check out, if he wished, the placement of her First Communion cross, since her uniform shirt was open to the full extent that the collar would allow. "Hi, kids," she said.

"It's nice of you, Melody," Slater said, "but really the kids can't accept — "

"Oh, I didn't buy them." She laughed. "It's a promotion. All the kids that get Happy Meals get sundaes."

"Oh," Slater said. He looked at Jilly, at Mickey and Veron-ica.

"Free, Daddy," Jilly said.

"Well, I guess it's O.K.," he said.

"So, how *are* you, Slater?" Melody said, still hanging around.

"Pretty good, pretty good." He put his hamburger down.

"Just a sec," Melody said. "I'll go get a cup of coffee and be right back."

"Don't you have to work?" Slater asked.

"Break time," she called back over her shoulder.

Looking around, Slater could see her arguing with one of the other women behind the counter. He slumped down in his seat and watched the kids eat — Jilly primly, Mickey intently, Veronica distractedly, but all of them fast, one eye on the sundaes that sat before them, melting slowly.

"No problem," Melody said, coming back. She chose to sit in the booth behind Slater so that he had to twist around to talk to her. She sat with her legs outstretched on the seat, back against the window, one arm on the back of the seat between them, her fingertips less than an inch from Slater's shoulder. "So is everything O.K.?"

"Pretty much," Slater said. He gave up on his hamburger and opened his coffee and blew across the surface of it, concentrating on its steam and blackness.

"I mean, really."

"Well," Slater said. It occurred to him that Kendra had talked to Melody about him. He looked at Melody, trying out this possibility. What did she know? Had Kendra said anything about how he could be when he got tired and then mad for no reason? (He knew that he did this.) Had she complained, as she had done to him, that he didn't help out enough, that he didn't even know where the coffee or the dishwashing soap or the big serving spoon was kept? He'd

said to her, How can you just flat leave your own children?
I don't see how you can do that. And she'd said she wasn't
deserting them, what she was doing was leaving them tempo-
rarily in their father's company, their own father, and he in
theirs. He wasn't a monster, was he? she'd said. Should she
get a babysitter? Should she call up Helen? She'd said this
very nicely, very quietly.

Had she talked to Melody about their private things,
maybe? But no, he thought, Kendra would never do such a
thing, never. He almost smiled, to think of her principles,
her rectitude, of her face in church — serious and beautiful,
dimples smoothed out, a dent between her eyebrows. But
then, he had never thought that she would leave him, and
she had. He knew she would not leave her children for good.
But her husband? She had her own ideas of what was right,
and he'd come up short of them.

"What the problem is, Melody . . ." he paused.

"Yes?" she said, leaning forward a little.

"The problem is that we've got to get this pumpkin. Right
away. Today. Now, Helen says that the place to go is the
produce and ice-cream stand over on Memphis. But I'd like
your opinion."

....

"Dad?" Jilly said to him.

"Hmm?" He was looking at every left-branching street for
the turnoff to the farmer's market Melody had recommended.

"We have to do a family tree for Monday."

"A what?" Melody had been annoyed with him. Melody
had also bumped him with her hip when she slid out of her

side of the booth. Slater considered these things with some satisfaction. He saw himself holding up his purity to Kendra in some possible future conversation. *You* left, he would say to Kendra, not me. I had nothing to do with a woman all the while you were gone (but how long would this be? he wondered) and you, he would say to her, who knows what you were doing?

"A family tree. For school. All our relatives and where everybody came from in Europe or wherever."

"Sounds very interesting," Slater said, taking the turnoff a little too fast.

"So I need to ask you some questions."

Slater stopped at a red light and turned around to look at Jilly. She was sitting straight as a die in the middle of the backseat, notebook propped up on her lap, pencil poised to write.

"What kind of questions?"

"Like the names of your father and your mother and all your brothers and sisters."

"Well," Slater said. He tilted his head back against the headrest. "That would be John William Slater, my father, and Rose Louise was my mother, and then there was me, then Paul — your Uncle Paulie — and Ruth and Donna and Kathy, Katherine, that is."

"What was Grandma's maiden name?"

"What?" Slater said, stalling, looking out at the deeply blue sky.

"Maiden name."

"Oh, maiden name. Well, let's see, I think it was something began with an O — was it Ostersomething?"

"*Daddy*," Jilly said. "Don't you even know your own mother's maiden name?"

Slater looked at the little wispy clouds in the sky for help. "Ostrowski," he said. "It was Ostrowski."

Jilly sat with her pencil unmoving. "Are you sure?"

"Of course I'm sure," he said.

"All right."

"Say, you guys, you see those dogs over there?" Slater indicated some providential dogs looming up beside the highway, leaping around their owner, who was raking leaves. "Those are Dalmatian type of dogs. Like in the movie."

Mickey and Veronica both looked at the dogs, but Jilly could not be led astray. "And what about your grandparents?" she said.

"Well, that'd be Charles and Mary Lou on my father's side," he answered quickly.

"What about on Grandma's side?"

"Well," he said. "Well, I'm not sure if I remember. I mean I'm not sure if anybody ever mentioned their names."

"Oh, Daddy." There was a world of disappointment in Jilly's voice, that instrument of destruction.

"They were dead already, you know, when I was a baby," Slater said, but he could see that it didn't make any difference to her.

They drove on in silence. Jilly had put her notebook away. Mickey and Veronica looked out their windows, barely moving. When they came to the sign for the farmer's market, Slater was so relieved that he wanted to put his head down on the steering wheel, just to rest it there for a minute with his eyes closed. But he turned the ignition off and opened his door, then opened all the doors, shepherding everyone out with smiles and cheerful comments. Ahead of them was a pile of pumpkins as big as a two-car garage, all sizes, knobby, smooth, cylindrical, round as the moon, twisted like the face of some old witch.

The kids ran on ahead. That's right, he silently admonished them, leave your old dad all alone, and that's how he did feel, alone, far behind the running of his children, their feet moving together like a dance, alone in one spot in the world by this barn and these pumpkins, so improbably in the middle of the city, so far from the spot where Kendra was just now. He walked on slowly. They were up on a ridge that once must have marked the edge of the city, although the city now sprawled far beyond it. This barn would have been here a long time, he thought, old wood, old beams holding it up, built by some man, now dead or impossibly old, for some woman who fed chickens here, swinging her arm in wide arcs as he had seen his grandmother Mary Lou do on their farm. Gone now, that old man and his old wife. And their family land a sort of bastard farm where people like him with no roots or wife could come for pumpkins or birdseed or flats of little no-account flowers, bright and with no scent.

When he got up close to the pumpkin pile, Mickey and Jilly each had their arms around one of the biggest orange suckers you could imagine. Veronica was holding a tiny one in her two hands and sitting on another as big as a foreign car. Jilly's arms looked so skinny, he thought, strained around the solid sides of the pumpkin.

"You may absolutely not have more than one," he said, lowering his eyebrows.

They looked at him, hardening their hearts against him, he

could see, and he held on to this feeling for a minute, so that
he should remember it. They held tighter than ever to their
choices, their noses and cheeks red from the wind, ears un-
covered, thin necks rising out of their collars, unprotected by
mufflers. These are motherless children, he said to himself.
I'm a man without a woman.

"Absolutely not more than one each," he said, and waited
for their happiness, but still they looked at him distrustfully.

"We *each* get one?" Mickey said.

"Yep."

"Any one at all?"

"That's right."

"Can we have two each?" Veronica asked, but the older
two shushed her while Slater turned, laughing to himself and
pretending not to notice.

On the way back, the kids argued in the backseat over
whose pumpkin was the biggest, but Slater paid no attention.
He had plans. He listed in his mind all that he would say to
Kendra when he called her. He would summon her from
down there at her mother's place like a singer with a love
song. He would describe the cemetery to her, the breadboard.
He would tell her stories about Halloween doings that had
happened in his family, how his father and his brothers had
taken a car apart and put it back together on the school
roof, how his grandfather had locked the preacher in his own
outhouse, how his grandmother, the one whose name he
couldn't remember, had crouched on a bridge with her girl
cousins and a dead snake and waited for an open-topped car
to come by. This would be casual, he thought. He would
mention how he might be lonely, how she might be. He
would say he'd done some deep thinking. Oh, have you? she

would say. I have, he would answer. He would wait for some
right moment, when he could gauge what she was feeling,
and then he would pop the big one.

So, when are you coming back?

I'm thinking about it. I am thinking about it — that would
be what she must say in order for the world to go on, and
his plan was to say anything, do anything at all to get her to
say it.

TRUE STORIES

::

It seems to me that there is in the world only death on the one hand, and on the other, frivolity. You're laughing, you're falling on the floor — death, you say, what a card, do you believe him? But listen. If you want to be taken seriously, if you want *important*, something for the long run: death. Anything else is high jinks, lacy underwear, material for low conversation over drinks.

This is the thing. If I told you I was over my buddy's house last week and I was leaving after a few beers, I'm pulling out the driveway slow and careful in preparation for a long finicking ride home watching the speed limit and the stop signs and just as I draw level with the sidewalk I look out the window of my truck and I see this woman walking toward me with quick long strides and she is the most beautiful woman I have ever seen in my life, long hair that blows back from her face, long legs crossing with every step, long fingers that she uses to comb through her hair, and I stop the truck to just look at her coming toward me and she walks right up to me and puts her one hand on the rim of the open window, curling her long fingers over the edge, and with the other hand she pushes the hair back from her face and she smiles and says to me with these big pouty lips, "You're cute." And then she goes around the front of the truck, wink — in my headlights, wink — out into the dark, and she's gone. So if I told you that, what'd you say? You'd laugh. Am I right?

Or what if I told you I stuck my head in my closet the other day looking for my old sweatpants that I haven't seen for six months but I keep looking for them every once in a while because they were the best ones I ever had — just the right feel against the skin, worn enough so that the elastic had some give — and while I'm in there rooting around in stuff I looked through before, sticking my hand in boxes and pushing back the swags of clothes hanging up, I hear a noise over my head of sliding, a clothy noise, and I look up and my gray '40s movie hat that my cousin Marie gave me for my twenty-first birthday fell down right on my head. I went and looked at myself in the mirror and the slant was just right, I could have went out on the town right then and there. If I told you that, you'd laugh. You'd shake your head and smile.

But wait. What if I told you I was out for a walk, maybe I was walking around looking for the long-legs long-haired woman, or maybe not, but I'm out walking along Pearl Road and I'm looking in all the windows of the stores but there's nothing doing because it's night, late, and all there is in there is the light they leave on so if anybody robs them the police will be able to see them at it if they drive by, and I'm looking in all the yards at the stiff little bushes and the lawns gray and spiky in the streetlight glare, and I'm looking at stuff along the curb, the old wrappers from Popsicles and bottle tops and combs with missing teeth and sometimes a sock or even a flattened shoe, and then I see — and this stops me cold — what seems at first like a fur hat, and then like a stuffed animal that some kid is missing, but what is really a cat curled in a coil like the letter C at the base of a phone pole, all the life gone out of it so that it is flatter somehow, its fur sticking out all anyhow like a bad toupee. Ha! No laughing now. No smiles. And that's just a cat, a fucking cat. The deadness of it. The uncatness of it. If that cat hasn't made it to spirit, hasn't gone to come back as grass or a pharmacist, gone to burn or play the harp with golden claws, it's nowhere, certainly no room in that fur piece for anything live. Well, I leave you to your beliefs.

So you see what I mean? Death, or who cares? Now the real story here is this, is how I figured this out. It has to do with women. Ask a woman what she wants in a man and one of the things she will always say is that she wants a man who will talk to her, who will tell her things. I want to know the truth (imagine me saying this in a high voice), she'll say. Sensitive too, good forearms, some preference for hair and eyes of this or that color, a nice butt some are looking for, but truth is right up there on the list. I'm not saying they don't mean it. I'm saying it doesn't work. The story is how I used to meet women in wherever — the bars or over somebody's house or at my sister's beauty shop — and keeping this truth thing in mind, and even because I'm naturally a truthful sort of guy in an equal situation, I'd say when it came up that I wasn't married. This is important to a woman, as is natural. But I used to be married. This is like to say — there's nothing wrong with me. Available but proven. And then they might say (imagine the high voice again), Oh, you were married? and they'd sort of trail the end of the sentence off like an invitation and that invitation reads, tell me about it. So I'd give them the story and the story is this.

I've been married five times, I'd say. Pause for expressions of awe or pity. Yes, five times. I'm thirty years old and I've taken vows five times. Then they look at me with this look and they say, how did that happen? And they're thinking, what a flirt, what a light type of guy. They see me picking up women and discarding them on a whim, because they don't buy the right kind of peanut butter or because their blouse is wrinkled when I take them to meet my Aunt Hattie or because they won't do something I want in bed. So I hasten to set this straight. Wasn't my idea, I say. I wanted marriage and all that goes with it. I'm easy to please. Beef Stroganoff or TV dinners on the table, either one and I'm happy. I can take it if the toothpaste tube is rolled up or twisted. There is no wrong way to have the toilet paper unroll as far as I'm concerned. In bed I'm Mr. Amiable, I'm so happy to be there with the woman I love, I'd do anything she said, and I'd do it twice. Three times. All I ever wanted was a true monogamous relationship. A true marriage, faithful, until death do us part. It was them that was unfaithful. Every one of the five of them was unfaithful to me. The first was unfaithful a year and a month after we married, in our own bed that we bought as part of a suite, with the guy who catered her sister's wedding. He was an old family friend. I was willing to forgive and forget, but no, she'd had a taste of freedom and she hardly stayed to pack. The second waited only six months before she left me for a guy in a local country band who she'd gone out with before we got together. He was going on tour to an assortment of western states, including Alaska to play for the guys who work on the pipeline, and she saw this as romantic.

Which it could be, I can see that. The third. She came home one day not wearing any underwear and when I asked about what she'd been doing that she'd felt she didn't need her bra and underpants for, she screamed and she threw dishes at me and she cried and said she was no good and then she left. The fourth I think never left off screwing around when we got married and so was never faithful and therefore could not be un. The fifth was the nicest. She was older than me by five years and she and I loved each other for what seemed like it might be a long time lasting even longer. She was settled — slow to talk, slow to move. Her hand cupping my shoulder, flattening out on my back, slow, moving down . . . Well. But after we'd been married three years she sat me down one day when I came home from work and said she was sorry but it was over. She'd met someone else and she hadn't slept with him but she was going to and she was sorry, but that was it. I appreciated her attitude and her method, but it was hard to take anyway.

So that's my story, and I tell it if it's required, to these women I meet, and you know what? They don't believe me. They look me up and down and smile. Five, they say. All unfaithful. You were the one who wanted to stay married. Hmmm. They're thinking, what's wrong with you, buster? Everything O.K. down there? What're you hiding? They're not buying it. They aren't impressed. They're looking around the bar or the basement of my buddy's house or my sister's beauty shop to see if there's anybody they can raise their eyebrows at like to say, do you believe this guy? And every word of it the truth, and not the kind of truth that you'd like anybody to laugh at.

So you're laughing now. At the story, sure. And to say,

what's with this guy, we've seen you with women, looking
for number six we suppose. And it's true that if I never find
the woman with the long fingers combing her long hair that
I'll have some other few to choose from. And the reason is
this. I have another story. This story is not my story. It's my
grandparents' story and it's a story I have a great respect for.
I don't tell it lightly. I tell it to a woman if I think we might
have something. Don't think I'm pushing for that sixth set
of wedding bands without a thought to the future in my
head. The sixth time is going to be the charm for me, the last
one, the final one. Maybe I haven't even told this whole
story to any woman yet, just the first sentence or two, or a
paragraph of it, just enough to let her know that I'm a serious
person. Maybe that was enough so far. Maybe I won't tell it
to anyone unless I find that woman with her long legs crossing
and recrossing, in boots, I'm almost sure she was wearing
boots. But anyway this is it, and you'll see that it proves my
theory.

My grandparents married when they were young, really
young. He was nineteen — Joseph. She was Victoria, sixteen.
That's how they did it in the old country. You got it out of
the way and then you stuck with it. But they didn't just stick
with it. They were in love, even as old as they were when I
knew them. She wore her hair the way he liked it, the way he
said he liked it when they met in 1926. He grew a mustache to
please her in 1933 and never shaved it off again. She made
halupke — stuffed cabbage — for him even though she hated
the smell of cabbage cooking. He braided her hair for her
every night, him sitting on the bed, her kneeling on the floor
between his knees. When he wanted to tease he'd call her
Cutie D'Amour which, he explained to me, was the name of

a cute showgirl in a Jimmy Cagney movie, whether the one with the grapefruit I'm not sure. It was a joke between them, a forty-year-old joke that they both still laughed at. So that's how it was with them. They were a joke themselves, they were so happy. When someone in the family got married, one of the toasts would always be that they should be as happy and for as long as Joseph and Victoria. My grandmother's legs got bad when she got older, in her seventies — I don't know what it was — from her diabetes maybe? I don't know — and my grandfather wouldn't let her do a thing. She couldn't dance anymore, was one thing. And he loved to dance, he loved it. He was a hell of a dancer, too, moving over the floor like skating. But she couldn't dance, so he said he wouldn't either. She tried to make him, but he refused. If she couldn't dance, for him, he said, it was like there *was* no one to dance with. He carried her up the stairs at night. There wasn't anything he wouldn't do.

So there was this one time, they'd had a long day. They went to this school play that my sister's daughter was in, their oldest grandchild. It was her eighth-grade play, what it was I don't even know, except that my sister's daughter, my niece, was in it and for her costume she wore her mother's prom dress, nipped in at the waist a little. My sister's husband told me this, after. How a bunch of the girls were wearing their mother's prom dresses, pinched in or let out as necessary. It was something to break your heart, my sister's husband said, the way these girls were so young in all this net and lace, their tits small and loose in their dresses, not filling out their bodices. It made him clear his throat several times, he said, to relieve the pressure of emotion. And my grandfather and grandmother were there, my grandmother in a wheelchair in the aisle, their eyes probably misting up, probably they were holding hands, or not actually holding — what they would do is my grandmother would put out her hand, palm down, and my grandfather would put his on top of it. And they went home, driven by my sister's husband. But when they got there, she felt a little funny, the excitement, dinner at the wrong hour, something. But anyway, she was having a spell, what she called a spell, that was her diabetes acting up. So they were going to take her to emergency, not that it was bad or anything, but just because the doctor said not to take chances. So my sister's husband is going to drive them there so she doesn't have to get out of the car. But then my grandfather says he'll take his car too, so my sister's husband doesn't have to wait around at the hospital. So O.K. My grandfather goes back into the house, who knows for what? To get his coat or blow his nose or any one of those dumb things you do every day and he's coming out of the house and he has a heart attack right on the doorstep, he's lying half in and half out of the door where one of the neighbors sees him and calls the ambulance. And he goes to the hospital. But he dies on the way. He's dead when he gets there. And they have to tell my grandmother. You don't want to see him now, they say to her. Calm yourself. Here, have some coffee. But she insists. She makes them take her down there where he is. Where he isn't. And when she sees him, when she sees his body, she makes a leap, a great lunge from her wheelchair and lies across his body. Take me with you, Joseph, she says. She screams it. And they pull her back into her wheelchair, this kind of behavior in old ladies is upsetting. Take me with you, Joseph, she yells, turning her head back, twisting around in her chair as they wheel her away. Take me with you. And

they admit her. And they put her up in a room. And she dies,
just like a promise. Half an hour later than my grandfather.
Maybe forty-five minutes. At the funeral, we had both their
coffins side by side in the center aisle of the church, draped
in white, and we put their wedding picture up between them,
how they looked fifty-seven years before, stiff, you know, but
pleased. And really, no one was very sad.

When I tell this story, which if I told all or part of, do you
see anyone smiling? Do you see anyone hiding their disbelief
behind their hands? Everyone recognizes the right stuff, the
good stuff when they hear it. It's like a gun, this story, a secret
weapon that I've got trained on the future. I'm waiting. I've
got my eye on death and all that goes before it and this time
I'm serious.

FIVE YEARS

I'm nothing, I'm nobody. This is what I said to myself on my way into the VFW hall, like a charm to keep myself steady, but really I was all right. I drove there in my own car and when I walked in I saw my own friends and family sitting at tables and standing around by the bandstand and getting drinks from the bar. "Give me a drink, quick, John," I said, and he laughed, and he did.

That was how the night started.

It was the Veterans Day dinner dance, which is the event that draws the most people at the VFW, although it's not as fancy as New Year's. It's a heavy thing to go to, a burden and a responsibility. Everyone drinks a lot. It was cool outside this time around — maybe starting to be chilly, but not cold.

"You're looking good," my cousin John said when he brought me a bourbon-and-Coke.

I kissed him, because why not, and I went over to sit with my Aunt Lou and her second husband, Eugene, and her kids.

"How are you, Kathy?" she asked me, and I said, "Just fine. How are you all?"

"Eugene's O.K., aren't you?" she said to him.

"Pretty good, pretty good," he said. "You're looking good, honey," he said to me.

"Well, I try," I said.

"What color is your nail polish?" the fourteen-year-old asked. She's Aunt Lou's oldest — the one she had with her dead husband.

"Strawberry Sherbet," I said, spreading my fingers out like a fan.

"Yum yum," the twins said together, and smacked their lips. They're Eugene's.

"They're going to be putting out the food in a minute," Aunt Lou said. "Where's your mom and dad?"

"They're not coming till later," I said.

"Well, I hope they're here in time for the door prizes."

I looked around to see who was there and it was the usual crowd. I could see Lisa and Jeannette sitting with their husbands. I could see John by the bar talking to some guys. I'd gone out with one of them a couple of months ago, so I waved. He waved back and crooked his finger for me to come over, but I just smiled and shook my head. So he started walking over to the table.

"Don't you need a drink?" he said to me.

"Do I?" I said. I had half left of what John had given me.

"Sure you do," he said.

I picked up my glass and drank the rest. "I guess I do," I said.

"So come on," he said, and I got up and walked to the bar with him. His hand was sort of hovering around looking for a place to rest, but I slid away from it.

At the bar they were telling stories.

"So the cop gets out of the car," John was saying, "and he walks up kind of slow and Big Ed's trying to push the gun in the glove compartment but it won't close and Joey's in the back going 'What'd you want to carry that gun in the car? Couldn't leave it at home, could you?' He was carrying on like an old woman, and Big Ed's swearing and trying to make the catch click — he kept hitting it with his hand — and I'm trying to be real cool."

"Ed's a nut about those guns," somebody said.

"He's certifiable," said Joey. "Anybody'd be upset."

"So then," said John, "the cop comes up by the car and I roll down the window and I say in this voice that kind of squeaks, 'What's the problem, Officer?' and he leans down by the window and says, 'Did you know that your taillights are out?' And right then the gun falls out of the glove compartment onto Big Ed's foot and he kind of yelps, and the cop says, 'What was that?' We thought we were dead."

"Give me another," I said to the bartender, who was this guy that my husband, Jake, went to high school with. He owns a dry cleaner's now. He's married to one of Jake's old girlfriends.

He poured from both bottles, showing off.

"Whoa," I said, because he was pouring pretty heavy.

"You've got to catch up," he said. "You look thirsty. Doesn't Kathy look thirsty?"

"She's gasping," John said. "Come on," he said to me, "I've got to go check up on the band."

So I went with him. I took a slug of my drink and it tasted really good, like it does on the nights when you're going to get blasted.

"You still going out with that loser?" John said when we got a little way from the bar.

"Shut up, John," I said. I wasn't anymore, but it wasn't his business. The band was set up, four skinny guys trying to look like the Eagles.

"You guys ready to start?" John said.

"We're on," the one with the cowboy hat said. "What do you want to hear?"

"How about something swingy so I can dance with this pretty lady?" John said.

"I'm his cousin," I said.

"How about 'Tequila Sunrise'?" he said.

So I set down my drink and John and I danced a fancy two-step.

"So how are you, Kathy?" he said to me.

"Oh, shut up."

"Not another word," he said.

"Is Eleanor here?"

"She's in the back getting the fried chicken and stuffed cabbage together."

"Is that what we're having?"

"Who knows?"

"So when are you and Eleanor going to have a baby?" I said to him.

"Gee, Granny Kathy, I don't know."

We danced on in silence. We were almost the only ones on the floor, because there's not many who want to do the two-step. Besides us, there were Mr. and Mrs. Kimball — eighty years old at least, but they were dancing like maniacs, their arms and legs and bodies moving together like friendly

machines, their faces perfectly calm, looking over each
other's shoulders like they'd been dancing for a hundred years
and could go on as long as they wanted. My second cousin
Angela was dancing with her fiancé, but they weren't doing
the two-step, they were just moving around. And there were
some kids sliding around and pretending to dance.

"I'm going to get drunk tonight," I said to John.

"Fine," he said.

"Blasted. Just drag me home at the end of the night."

"We'll do that."

"Or forget it, I'll find someone taller and stronger and not
related to me."

"That's O.K., too."

"Oh, shut up."

The band was supposed to play for fifteen minutes for
openers and then while everybody went up to the buffet and
ate, but they took a break right away when the food came
on. The band ate at a separate table over by the door to the
main bar, in the other room. I got another drink and sat with
Aunt Lou and Eugene and the kids while they ate. I was
thinking about — oh, I don't know, nothing much. I guess
about that dopey guy I wasn't going out with anymore, and
also about the one I was going out with now, who I hadn't
wanted to bring tonight, because I didn't like him well
enough to make him public. I was thinking about John some,
and how Eleanor was nice enough but not really what I
thought John would go for, but they seemed happy. I was
possibly thinking about Jake, but not much, not in a bad way.
I was just feeling the bourbon fizzing through my veins and
waiting to be high. I kidded around some with Aunt Lou's
three.

Then this woman came over. "Lou?" she said. "Is that you?" Some old girl she used to know before she was married to Eugene, someone from school.

"And are all these yours?" she said.

"Not me," I said.

"This my niece, Kathy. Kathy, you know Mrs. Weed."

"You must be Dave and Annie's girl, then." And I could see her remembering things about me.

"Nice to meet you," I said, getting up. "I seem to need another drink."

"I was terribly sorry to hear about your husband," she said, too quick for me.

"Me too," I said, swirling my drink in the glass.

"Well, I'll say a little prayer for him when I do my dead," Mrs. Weed said. She turned to Aunt Lou and said, "I pray for all my dead every Friday night, for Mother and Father and the little one — you know, the first one, that had the cord wrapped around his neck — and a lot more. I keep a list, and I'll put your Jake on it."

"Thanks," I said.

"How did it happen, dear?"

I didn't want to tell her. I hated to have to tell her. But there is a way to behave when you are with people that made me tell her, and also it was the nature of the day, which is a day for the dead and for the remembrance of the dead and of their stories.

"It was on a motorcycle. A car cut in front of him and he flipped it."

"Oh my, oh my. He was so young. It's the young like that that you just don't understand."

"Yes," I said.

I walked away holding my glass hard between my fingers, feeling the stiffness of my face. "Hit me again," I said to the bartender.

Lisa came up behind me and draped her arm around my neck. "You want to fast dance if they play something good?" she said.

"I need at least two more drinks," I said.

"Bartender," she called. "Two more drinks, here. This woman needs to dance."

"What do you want?" he said.

"You want to do some shots?" I asked. "Where's Jeannette?"

"There she is," Lisa said, and we both waved at her to come over.

We all had a shot. Lisa had peach schnapps, Jeannette had Amaretto, I had Yukon.

"To men," I said.

"To great hair," Jeannette said.

"To oral sex," Lisa said.

"Lisa, you're disgusting," Jeannette said, laughing.

"I'm serious. This is a serious toast. Call that bartender back over here and ask him if he doesn't think oral sex is serious stuff."

We scuffled by the bar for a minute while Lisa pretended she was going to make the bartender come over.

"Stop it, you slut," I said.

"All right," Lisa said. "I'm cured. I'm going to just think about oral sex."

"Well, really, you know, I don't really like it. You know?" Jeannette said, lowering her voice.

"Don't like it?" Lisa said. "What does Ray have to say about that?"

"I just told him that I'd do it like maybe once in a while or whatever, but not all the time."

"Jeannette, you're such a prude," I said.

"Forget it, you guys," Jeannette knocked her shot back and set the glass on the counter. "Ray wouldn't like it if he knew I was talking about it anyway."

"Ray would love it," Lisa said. "Men love it if they think women are talking about them. That's why they get married, so they'll have a woman in a permanent position to talk about them. When I talk about my honey, I go home and tell him. It turns him on. I think you should tell Ray what we all said."

"Not in a million years."

"Well, Kathy and I'd be happy to do it for you. Wouldn't we, Kathy? We're all friends. I'll tell Ray, and you can tell Bill. It'll make them hot. Right, Kathy?"

"You scratch my back and I'll scratch yours," I said. Then she looked at me, and I could see her remembering. She looked at Jeannette and I could see them remembering together. I could see them wondering if I was thinking about Jake, or if I was sleeping with someone else and thinking about him, and I despised them for it, I wanted to scratch their faces and rip their clothes or my own for thinking those things about me, or anything about me at all.

I set my glass down. "I think this is my song," I said. "You'll have to excuse me." I walked carefully toward the john. It seemed a very long way. When I got there, I pissed, and then I began to wash my hands but only held them under the cold water. I took out my lipstick and did my lips over again, very carefully outlining the arch of the upper lip and the curve of the lower. I didn't have a comb, so I ran my fingers through my hair. I looked as good as I did when I was twenty. Better maybe. No one could ever tell how old I was. They always guessed twenty-one or maybe twenty-three. What I am is twenty-eight, so I had five years' leeway. Five free years, so to speak. Five years that had gone and didn't count. What had happened in them was nothing. It was zip. My legs were wobbly, but I hadn't drunk enough yet.

When I came out, the band was taking a break, so I went over and sat at their table. "Do you do any Alabama?" I asked the drummer.

"We do 'Lady Down on Love,' " he said.

"So would you do it for me?" I said.

"Sure," he said. He pulled the top of his beer, watching me through his bangs. He thought he was being really cool. "So are you a veteran?" he said.

"Only of love," I said.

"A veteran of love, that's good. Hey, Tim, that's you," he said to one of the other guys. "Tim just ran into this girl he used to be hung up on and got hung up all over again."

"Did she look just the same?" I asked him.

"She looked better," he said. He was a really hangdog guy. Everything about him drooped.

"So what'd you do?"

"Nothing," he said. He drank some beer. "She and I went together for a long time, and then, I don't know, she got funny about some things and she wanted to get married, and so all of a sudden what do I know but she goes and marries this guy from Texas and goes back to Texas with him, just like that. He had four kids already from someone else."

"So then what?" I said.

"So then I got married to this broad I met out playing, but it was on the rebound. I never really loved her."

"You don't look like you're old enough to have had time to do all that," I said to him.

"When I saw her again, it all came back."

"She still married?" I asked.

"Yeah. She's up visiting her mother. She brought two of those kids with her. The funny thing is, one of them looks just like her."

"That's it," the drummer said. "You can wait for the kid to grow up. Your problems are over." He turned to me. "So, are you here with somebody?"

"No," I said. "But you'd better watch out, because I'm related to half of the biggest guys here."

"Oh yeah? I'm sweating," he said. "What makes you think I got anything on my mind?"

"Just a hunch," I said.

"Well, stick around after," he said.

"Maybe I will," I said, and I got up and went to wander up and down the rows of tables.

"Over here, Kathy."

I sat down by Aunt Lou. She was sitting with some of the Ladies' Auxiliary and they were all criticizing the food. The piroshki were hard around the edges, they said. Too much salt in the scalloped potatoes. They ran out of whipped Jell-O.

"Who made that chocolate cake with the pink icing?" one of them said.

"That was Nettie Bill."

"No, it was Aunt Mary Farrell. I saw her bring it in."

"Well, the icing was rancid. I took a big bite and like to died."

"Nellie Bill got married along about the same time I got married to Jack," Aunt Lou said. "We used to run around together, the four of us."

"Oh, that Jack was a riot, he was a ripsnorter," another lady said.

"He could be wild," Aunt Lou said. "But still."

"Still?" I said.

"There was that time, you know," she said, nodding to the ladies, "when I was getting unengaged from that guy who worked at the mill and just starting with Jack. And I told him, the mill guy, that it was all over and that I was going to go with Jack, and he got so mad when I told him and he said he was coming over. My, but I was scared. Although I don't suppose now that he would have done anything. But anyway I called Jack and he came over and took me to the O.K. — you remember? — the O.K. Diner. That was what it was called then," she said to me. "Now it's something else. What is it? — the All-American Diner, I think. It's a lot cleaner now. But we went there and we talked and he bought me coffee and was just as nice. Oh, he dragged me through some awful times and I loved him through them all, because of things he did like that."

The ladies nodded. My head was buzzing. But I was not drunk yet.

"I'll never forget that, how he just came and took me away, didn't even ask any questions."

I got up and left them all staring into the middle distance. I didn't like it, this sense that other people's lives were rubbing up against me. I shook my hair and shrugged my shoulders. I smoothed down the sleeves of my dress.

Then it was time for the ceremonies. Old Mr. Kimball got up, wearing his World War II stuff, with that funny little folded hat. He started making some jokes, and I saw my parents come in. I waved but I didn't go over. They went and sat with Aunt Lou and Eugene. I sat down at the bar. I held out my glass and the bartender came and filled it up.

"And now," Mr. Kimball said, "our national anthem."

I set my glass on the bar and stood up with everyone else while we sang along with a record. The scratchy notes were like feathers in my ears, and they went scratching at the back of my throat. And then Mr. Kimball read the list of the dead. Each of the names was heavy, they fell from his mouth like fruit, solid and enclosed in a skin. I heard my Uncle Jack's name. I heard the name of my grandfather's brother. Of one of my father's best friends. Of the boy down the street, ten years older than me and ripe, then, for Vietnam. Vincent Miller. Henry Stacek. John Thomas Richlovsky. Lloyd Oliver. They didn't say Jake's name, of course. I reached behind me and put my hand on my drink. The glass was wet and cold. My lips were numb. I was almost drunk, but not quite.

Then they played "Taps" and I thought, how I hate this, how this makes my skin crawl. I looked around. One woman had her head bowed and was clutching the back of her chair, and another was standing up very straight, her jaw stuck out and wobbling. Some had faces like stone and some like the soft undersurface of the clouds before it rains. The men stood at attention, unbending their old bodies, and their eyes were on something far away that no one can see any longer. The music was so slow, each note so long.

Then, thank God, thank God, it was over. I drank from my glass and went looking for someone — John, I thought, or that drummer. But I ran into Aunt Lou's fourteen-year-old.

"Kathy," she said, "could you get me a drink, please?"

"Do you want pop or what?" I asked her.

"Not pop. A drink."

"What are you, kidding me?"

"I want to see what it's like. Come on, Kathy. Just a little one."

"O.K.," I said. "But wait here."

I went over to the bar and asked the bartender for a glass of cherry pop, and I brought it back to her. "Just make sure you drink it slow," I said. "And for God's sake, don't act silly." She took it and carried it away, holding it carefully in front of her.

I sat down right where I was, at an empty table. It was hot. I could see my parents and Aunt Lou and Eugene and the twins across the room, and John and Eleanor by the band-stand, and Lisa and Jeannette and their husbands dancing to a slow dance. But I didn't want to talk to any of them, I was tired of them and their stories.

I sat there and I started to think about Jake. This was dangerous, I knew, but I didn't care. I thought about him for a while, and then I started to feel strange, my head felt strange. I was thinking faster and faster, and it made me uncomfortable, but I tried on purpose to remember how he looked. I tried to imagine him sitting down in the chair next to me. I tried hard to imagine him, up from the pieces that were all I could bring back — his hair, his forehead with the hair falling across it, his arm in the sleeve of his gray workshirt, his hand with the sleeve rolled back from it holding a cup of coffee or a beer — and I couldn't. My head was floating and my brain felt wedged in too tight. I shivered like someone had touched the back of my neck with a cold finger. I shifted in my chair and looked around and I saw him, saw Jake, at the other end of the hall, twenty-five feet away, saw him from the back, turned away from me so that I could only see his jaw, his fingers twitching, holding a cigarette, but it was him. It was unmistakable the way his shirt was tucked into his pants, the shape of his head, the curve of his body leaning against the wall. He was looking through the door that led into the bar, and he was smoking, and then he pushed the door farther open and went through it and I didn't see him anymore.

I was ordering my legs, Get up! Get up! and flexing my fingers to hold on to the table and pull, stiffening my back, tensing my shoulders. Nothing worked like it should.

"Once the Crucifixion was just a story to me," a voice said in my ear. "No question of believing or not, it was said and I heard it. God was like my grandfathers."

I turned my head with great effort and saw that Mrs. Weed was looking at me from close up, looking right into my eyes.

"I'd never seen my grandfathers anyway, because they were both dead. And Jesus could have been my uncle, like the one who had gone to fight in the war and never came back, though he was listed as neither dead nor missing. All the big events — the changing of water to wine, the big scene in the temple, the Stations of the Cross, they were like family stories, you know what I mean?"

I nodded. My lips were still numb.

"But what I think is that we have the story of the Crucifixion to prepare us early for trouble in our life, trouble and pain. Life is pain and trouble, trouble and pain." She patted my hand, my cold hand that lay on the table in front of me like a clod of dirt.

"I had a vision," I told her, pushing each word through my stiff lips. "I saw him."

"Blessed be the Lord." She held my hand between hers. "I'll put you in my prayers."

"I'm not dead yet," I said. I took my hand away from her and got up.

Each step was hard, for my feet were stiff in their shoes. I walked the long way down the hall and went out the back into the cold night air. The yard was empty except for some old boxes and a portable barbecue grill that they did clams on for Labor Day. The moon was shining, dense and cold as perfume in the air. I would never go inside again, I decided. I would never live in a house again, would never sleep in a bed, never comb my hair in front of a mirror. I was drunk now. I knew all that.

MOMMY AND DORIS

::

I was sitting in McDonald's drinking decaf and making my shopping list last Thursday, in the afternoon, around maybe two-thirty. I vary my routine like they say you should so as to fool muggers, so I'm there all hours. Always the same day: Thursday, which I picked as my shopping day long ago because it's the day after the specials come out. But different times on Thursday.

The little girls behind the counter were relaxed. They were cleaning up some but mostly they were talking and laughing and making comments to the boys cooking up hamburgers at the grill. The day manager on Thursday is mean, I gather, but she spends a lot of time on the phone and up front trying to pick up customers, so mostly they don't mind her.

I had my first cup of decaf in front of me. It's even better than I make, to tell the truth, and they keep it coming. I don't mind like some do if I have to go up and get it myself. I hold out my cup and the girl comes over with the pot and she pours and I smile and she smiles. What's to complain about?

I had just poured my three creams into the cup and stirred

it all around with the end of my pen. I'd sat down midway between a mother with three little girls all in sunsuits and little white sandals and a lone man with his paper and a legal pad he was scribbling in. I got out my notebook. Ha, I thought, I can scribble, too, Mr. Blue Suit. I didn't like his attitude.

I always do my list there because if I do it at home I get so bored sitting at the kitchen table looking out at the blank wall of the house next door with the curtains pulled down to the exact six or however many inches from the sill that silly old Mabel thinks is right. But at McDonald's there is the smell of the french fries frying and the girls with their matching caps running back and forth behind the counter or leaning on it with their elbows bent almost backward. And there are the other people to watch, the mothers with their little kids and the fathers taking their boys out after softball and the women out together eating one of the sundaes — "I know I shouldn't," they say — and the men sitting alone and reading the paper. I like to watch them.

So I was sitting there in my half booth, watching Mr. Suit and the mother with her three girls who were all taking perfect tiny bites out of their hamburgers and sipping through their straws and dipping their french fries one by one into piles of ketchup that their mother had squeezed out for them. The boxes that their Happy Meals had come in were sitting in the middle of the table and the little girls had their eyes fixed on them while they chewed. I wrote down
Lemon Tea
Spray Starch
Granny Smith apples (3)
A man, a young man, and his two children came over and

sat down to my left. He carefully arranged them in their seats
with napkins which he let the older child, a girl, get from the
counter by herself. They all sat there, no food yet. He sat
with his arms stretched out on the table, as if he hoped to
contain them there against some future event. The little boy
wanted to get napkins too, so the father let him out to get
some more and then the two children separated the napkins
into thick piles which they divided and redivided. I wrote
down

Napkins — cheap

Kitchen matches

Peppercorns

Granola bars (crunchy)

"Daddy," the girl said, "where will Mommy and Doris
sit?"

"They will sit right here," he said. All three of them turned
to look at the counter.

"Aha," I thought, cocking my pencil. Mommy and Doris.
I glanced at Suit and the three little girls. They were still
doing the same things: scribbling, chewing, staring. Their
mother was dampening Kleenex in her glass of ice water and
wiping ketchup from the corners of their mouths. The girls
behind the counter were dancing around, waiting on a sudden
flux of customers, out of which I tried to pick Mommy and
Doris. I wrote on my list

Tomatoes (4)

which I need to buy early in the summer before my garden
starts producing and I can supply half the neighborhood,
heaping coals of fire on the heads of the neighbors I particularly dislike. It is for this reason alone that I grow zucchini,
which I detest.

I looked up. I had missed Mommy and Doris detaching themselves from the crowd and here they were distributing color-coded hamburger containers and Happy Meal boxes and drinks. They sat down, rearranging themselves. They had one of those split booths with two tables in an enclosed space, one that seats four and one that seats two. The man, the boy, and Mommy sat at the bigger table. Doris sat at the small table and the girl went to sit with her.

I have perfected this way of watching people without staring. It's my secret — don't think I'm not going to keep it that way. But it has to do with the angle of the eyes and the focus of your intent. There, that's all I'll say. Thank God I've still got my hearing. I know this makes me sound nosy. Well, I am nosy, and I don't care. I look on it as my right as an older woman, just as it is the right of a younger woman to attract the notice of men. What is life for if not to entertain us, after the more serious purposes are taken care of or you've decided against them?

I was taken with this family. They seemed careful. It seemed that they all, even the little boy, hesitated before performing the simplest actions. There was this tiny stop before they bit into their hamburgers or opened the bun to take the pickles out and lay them on the sides of their trays. They would look around at each other to check — check what? I wanted to know. And they were all interesting to look at, each in their own way. They made a list in my mind —

The father — dark hair, almost black, young-man skinniness that would fill out in a few years so that his shoulder blades didn't show under his shirt anymore, a white skin that flushed when he was hot or irritated, discontented around the eyes, confused at the mouth, hands that didn't know what to do with the smallness of his children's arms.

The mother — blond, with hard hair arranged in little bunches around her face, red mouth, slender and tough. Dyed, manicured, slashes of rouge up her cheeks, so you could see she had in mind to look like someone on TV, not that she looked bad, oh no, she looked like Lana Turner if you know who that is. But scary. All sharpness and angles. She looked like she wished McDonald's had knives, even those twisty plastic ones, so she could cut things in two.

The kids were like a set made to please wishing parents: one blond, one dark; one small and round and red-cheeked, grasping and climbing, reaching for packets of salt to spill; one long and coltish and smooth-skinned, twisting legs, looking down at her food, talking like an adult-in-training. A boy for you, a girl for me.

And Doris. Doris was a little overweight, a little soft, with lank smooth brown hair hanging out of its ponytail-holder, soft pink cheeks. Round face, soap-washed, you wanted to pinch it. Big brown eyes, long eyelashes — eyes like Bossy was what my brothers used to call them on the farm. Oh Doris, I wanted to say — sit up straight.

What was it about them all? I don't know. I lowered my head and wrote
Half carton eggs
2 sticks marg.

Did they love each other, this husband and wife? She looked so smooth-surfaced, so shiny, so crisp and pointy. When I tried to imagine them kissing I thought I saw her keeping her mouth closed over her small sharp teeth, fixing her hair after every hug. I watched with my sideways stare to see if he looked at her with love or longing.

And Doris. What about Doris? Doris, scraping the onions off the little girl's hamburger, a piece of her hair falling forward from behind her ear where she had hooked it. It seemed to me that she spent a lot of time with them all, for they didn't feel they had to talk with each other. Doris straightened the little girl's collar as if she was used to doing it and the little girl did not start when she felt Doris's fingers on her neck. But she was not related to them. She didn't look like any of them. The children didn't call her Aunt Doris. Doris, the family friend, then. The wife's friend from high school. They used to go to dances together, and the wife, then not a wife, would pick up with some boy and leave Doris to get home as best she could. Doris had gone to a lot of dances in high school where she leaned against the wall drinking small paper cups of Coke and watching the little bunches of hair pressed against different male shoulders. She should have minded this more than she did.

Chicken thighs, I wrote.

Bread crumbs

I slid my eyes left. Mr. Suit was gone, leaving his trash behind him, one of those that think they're doing working people a favor if they make them more work. He'd left his paper, I saw, and I considered going over and getting it — a free paper — why not? When I was younger I'd have been too embarrassed to take it, but there's nothing I wouldn't do now if I wanted to. Some teenage boys in leather jackets sat down just beyond where Suit had been sitting. Teenage boys are not interesting unless they get up to antics. The most they usually do is blow straws at each other or make salt and pepper drawings.

Taking a sip of my decaf, I looked back to see what Mommy and Doris were doing. The little boy had to go to the bathroom. He said it in that clear, loud voice children always use to say things like this, and with that same emphasis: "I *have* to go to the *bath*room." It's a sort of song they all learn, from the air, it seems like.

Toilet paper

I wrote down, and then considered. Didn't I have two rolls left? But then, it's something you're always going to need. But then again, I was a little short this week. I was pretty sure about the two rolls, so I crossed it out.

The boy was too young to go with his father to the men's room. I wondered if his mother would make Doris take him, but, no, it seemed that she was going to do it. There was some question of whether the little girl should go too.

"You'll just have to go later," her mother said.

"But I don't *have* to go now," she said, twisting her legs around.

"We're leaving right after we eat, so you better go now."

"I went at Grandma's."

"All right, but don't come crying to me when you can't hold it," her mother said and marched off, holding on to the little boy by his arm.

During all this, the father and Doris had said nothing, and I watched them more closely in the absence of the mother, whose sandal heels I could still hear tapping on the tile floor. He offered her a napkin now, from the pile the children had made. She took it, not looking at him. She wiped up some ketchup that had oozed off the little girl's hamburger paper, talking softly to her, shaking her head so that her soft hair fell down over her face. Her bangs were too long and she was not one of those girls who are good with a curling iron, you could tell. The father watched the two of them. His face was patchy, red-blotched. Finished with the napkin, Doris held it between her fingers for a minute, gingerly. He reached over and took it from her. He held it in the same way that she had, confused, and then he got up and walked to the trash can and threw it away.

I was watching them pretty closely now. It seemed to me that here was a part of the answer to "what about Doris?" He looked at her, I thought, with a caring eye. He flicked looks at her that made his cheeks burn redder. She stabbed the ketchup with her french fries.

"Daddy," the little girl said, "I want some McDonaldland cookies."

He pulled out his wallet and gave her a bill. "Get some for your brother," he said.

She got up and went toward the counter, walking in that way children do sometimes, dragging their feet for the pleasure of it, sliding their hands along the surfaces they come across to feel smooth, rough, prickly, dry, wet.

Oreos

Lorna Doones

I wrote, both of which keep good and are the favorites of Mabel next door, who, silly as she is, plays a good hand of gin rummy. I took another sip of decaf and sat up very straight, inclining myself as far toward the father and Doris as I could, imagining that I could focus my left ear to hear better.

Doris bent over to tie her shoe. She sat up and hooked the

hair that had flopped forward back behind her ears. He picked up the little boy's abandoned hamburger and took a bite out of it. He looked at her, or toward her, when her head was turned away. She put her hand to her neck, and then, quickly hooked her finger through her bra strap and pulled it back up onto her shoulder. She looked over at him where he was frowning down at his drink.

"Say, Doris," he said.

"What?" she said.

"You want some of these french fries?"

"No," she said. "I don't think so."

Come on, I said, mentally urging them. But they just sat there, looking at the bits of food left on the table, and then the little girl came back with the boxes of cookies and the mother came tapping back from the bathroom, holding the little boy by his arm, his face now red and shiny, from crying and being washed.

I could have cried myself, really. That is how silly I was. So I set myself to my shopping list, which was almost done.

Prunes, pitted

Vanilla extract

Iced raisin bars

Notepad

Bottle Gallo chablis

They were getting things together to leave, gathering up their papers and Styrofoam containers onto the trays, looking for the little girl's barrette that had slipped out of her fine, shiny hair, tying the trailing lace of the little boy's shoe. What a to-do there would be, I said to myself, if I went over and told them what I thought, if I took Doris aside and said, "Ask more from life," or said to the father, "Stop torturing her —

shit or get off the pot," or to the mother, " — ." But what can you say to a woman like that?

Doris was herding the kids before her, helping them with their trays, carrying the Happy Meal boxes, and I could see how all her days and nights went. I could see how the mother would call her up to babysit with no notice and not even leave her a six-pack or a bag of chips to console herself with, how she would live on glances from the father, wait for times when he said he liked her blouse or brushed up against her in the hall when she was putting the children to bed at a party given by the mother. She would always be ready to drop everything and come over, because of her sweet nature and on the chance of seeing him. And him, what would he do? He might — some night when he and his sharp little blond wife were out at the movies or the bar, excuse himself in the middle of a dull love scene or while she was flirting with the bartender — he might call the radio station that he knew Doris listened to when she was babysitting and dedicate a song: "To Doris from someone who cares." And consider himself a romantic, a hell of a yearning and moral fellow, up to here with fine feelings.

I watched them walk out to the car and get in, Doris sitting in the backseat in the middle, between the two children. I looked around McDonald's. The little girls drooped in their uniforms behind the counter. It was the slow of the afternoon. The mean day manager was sitting out front with a priest, leaning forward, talking to him eagerly, a secular sort of confession maybe, telling him all the meannesses of the day that she had inflicted on the girls behind the counter, how she had forced them to clean the stainless a second time because of one spot, how she made one cry by telling her she

looked fat in her uniform pants, how she fired another for a
shortage in her drawer when all the time it was she herself
who had taken out change for a ten. Whatever she was saying,
the priest sat looking serious, nodding, drinking his coffee in
little sips. He was a priest. He would have to forgive her.

It was time to go shopping. If I waited much longer, the
store would be full of after-work shoppers, flying in on their
way from the office or the factory to get frozen burritos or
some Shake 'n Bake and a frozen cherry pie for dinner. But
still I sat, looking at the sad vision of Doris in her sad sleeveless
blouse, her black scuffed oxfords. It wasn't my own life I was
looking at, don't think it. Even if there doesn't seem to be
much in it, gin rummy and a little bingo with Mabel, a chat
with the mailman, a postcard and a visit from my cousin once
a year — even if there isn't much, it's not me I'm sorry for.

I was unhappy, though, unsettled, heavy in my seat, too
heavy-feeling to get up and go as I ought to walk behind the
shopping cart in the Pick-n-Pay. But this is what being old
teaches you: do something about it, or forget it. I didn't want
to forget about Doris.

Doris, I said to her in my mind, staring ahead as if I could
see her, as I almost could. Doris, I said. And I made myself
see what could happen to her that would be good.

Would Doris get a boyfriend? They both, the father and
the mother, would mind, for different reasons, but surely one
day she must. Some man will look at her and see how her
skin is pink and white, notice how her hair lies smooth like
ribbons against it, how she looks up from under her eyelashes.
Doris will meet him when she has broken a shoelace in her
ugly black shoes that she so persistently wears with white
ankle socks. She will be barefoot maybe, standing in the lawn

holding the sprinkler over the dancing children that she is babysitting once again, and this man will be driving down the street or walking past on the sidewalk, or he will be the repairman that the mother, Doris's good friend, said surely Doris wouldn't mind letting in the house while she and the father go to a movie/dancing/dinner with the boss. Doris will look at him and he will see her worth. He will take her and the children for a ride in his repairman truck. He will buy them all ice cream, and when they come back to the house, she will hand the children over to their parents who will have come back in the meantime, puzzled but not worried because of course Doris remembered to leave them a note, and he will take her away in the truck while they stand staring, lined up in front of the house like lawn ornaments, the father blotching up scarlet in the face, the mother shaking her hard little bunches of hair, the children scraping the ground with the toes of their sneakers and calling for Doris to come back to play Candyland. But she will be gone.

You hear that, Doris? I said in my mind. And then I got up and slid the cup and napkins and cream containers from my tray into the trash container, settled my purse on my shoulder, picked up my list, and went shopping.

THE LIFE OF
THE BODY

::

I was cutting up asparagus in the sun from the kitchen window and listening to heavy-metal music with my second-born, my jelly doughnut, while my firstborn, the angel-child, sulked in the dining room and was therefore on hand to take the fateful phone call. I kept cutting asparagus — two cuts each, one to cut off the pale callused end, another to separate the crispy middle from the tender spear. I did them individually, searching on each one with my knife for the invisible places that divide asparagus into three parts. When I took the phone from my unsmiling daughter my hand was wet with asparagus water.

"Guess what," the phone said, and I said, "What, Markie," in an exaggerated way to amuse Claudia, who was standing there still sulky but with signs of wanting attention. At the same time I hoped to annoy my sister by calling her Markie, which no one mostly did anymore, because here we were again — me with my hands in food and her calling up with excitements.

"Roman is back," she said. I had a strong desire to act out: to wail, or plunge the knife still green with asparagus fibers into the imitation butcher-block counter in front of me. It was resilient and soft enough to make this a satisfying experience. But I resisted because Claudia and Vicky were watching.

Mostly Markie and I had not found the same men attractive. I like them beefy and blond, with light eyes: blue or gray. She goes for the intense, troubled, volatile ones, no particular color scheme, although they have tended to be dark. It's worked out quite well. But Roman was neither of these types. He had dark-red hair, was cheerful with philosophical moments, had really great forearms and a plan to save the world. He'd looked wonderful in denim and had one dark and one light eye.

What about the universe anyway? Does it end? Is there a floor or ceiling? And this cyclical stuff I read about in the science column of the daily paper — everything is going to happen all over again? Or it happens all over again but backward? I'd like to be able to give Claudia and Vicky a hint about this before it's too late. Stop now, I'll tell them. Think about this boy at forty. Do you want to go through this again? I resisted the knife, but allowed myself to press my wet fingers to the ridge of bone over my right eye.

"What's he doing back?" I asked. "What'd he come back here for?" If it had been Claudia saying this I would have told her to stop that whining or else.

"He's giving a reading to benefit his high school."

"Jesus," I said. Claudia mouthed "Jesus" to Vicky who

snickered. "Go away," I said to them and they put on their come-on-Mom faces.

"We have to see him, Kate," said Markie.

"Oh no we don't."

"Admit it — wouldn't you like to see him?"

I turned away from Claudia and Vicky and whispered into the phone: "No, I wouldn't. I wouldn't. Absolutely not. No."

"I don't believe you. Put some coffee on and I'll come over and we can talk about it."

"Coffee, O.K. Talk, O.K."

"You know you'd like to see him."

"From a distance maybe."

"Besides, I want to get the letters back and I don't want to do it alone. You have to come with me."

"Get what back?"

"The letters. Those letters I wrote him — you remember?"

. . . .

I made coffee without even washing the asparagus water off my hands, a detail pointed out to me by Claudia who ostentatiously wiped a small green smear off the coffeepot. I did remember the letters, they were not what I didn't want to remember, which was the awesome miasma of feelings I had felt when I was involved with Roman. How awful he made me feel. Crying in public on the mall by the fountain. How I called up his sister and had to hear from her that he had dumped me. His thing about freedom that I had been unable to resist the logic of at the time. Even worse: how wonderful the charm of his favor, his smile; how I would wait for him at one of our meeting places with the most marvelous irreplaceable sense of happiness and expectation.

Now I see that, aside from the fact that he was in some ways a jerk, all this was caused by the irresistible logic of the body — it turns toward or it turns away, and you can justify or analyze but in the end it makes no difference. Either you follow and are happy, at least for a while, or you don't and are miserable, until your mind has time to catch up and create a new possible universe.

But wait, I said to myself as the coffee dripped in a steady stream, everything is different. That is the past. The present is me married to Dak in a pretty O.K. way, with the happy annoyance of Claudia and Vicky.

Blandly, the facts are these: Markie and I both went out with Roman — not at the same time — and he dumped both of us. He dumped Markie twice actually, but this reflects no credit on me. My passion for him was anyway less pure.

Visions of high school: plaid skirts, regulation blouses, hair and makeup inspections. Markie went out with Roman first, when she was fifteen and he was seventeen. He was her first date, in fact. They went bowling and she dropped the ball on his transistor radio. But they went out for a bit and Markie developed an intense unserious crush on him which went on sort of happily (on her part at least) until she asked him to the junior/senior prom and he said no. This happened when I was thirteen, during a period when Markie and I were not getting along well, so I didn't get the details. Now, with an adult perspective, we can see that she had been assuming a lot, but then she was dumb and young and pretty upset.

Then I was sixteen and I met Roman again at a party that he was really too old for, being now twenty. I loved him right away for being old, for having a glamorous job as an insurance detective, because he wrote poetry (although I didn't know

then that he was going to make a career out of it), and because
he was Markie's old boyfriend. I liked that part of it almost
best. Markie had lost him, I thought, but I would do better.
I was the new generation. I had my head together.

I looked back then to the times I had seen Roman before
and reconstructed them. For instance: the party where I first
met him. Markie took our cousin Carol Ann and me, both
underage, and we got raided by the police. (We hid beer
cans under the wastebasket. We thought it was wonderful.) I
looked back at this and thought how, at this first sight, Roman
had really loved me, but knew I was too young and had to
be satisfied with Markie. I said phrases over to myself like,
"He saw her and said to himself, 'This is the girl I'm going
to marry.'" I remember with awe the sense that my sixteen-
year-old self had of my thirteen-year-old body as pristine and
prize-able, something that had hardly to be offered for it to
be desired.

But he did to me what he did to Markie, only he strung
me along for a year instead of three months.

And finally Markie had a cautious affair with him after her
husband, Len, died, pretty much a rebound thing, and this is
when the letters date from. They are part letters, part poems
that she wrote him when he left town to take a job at a
college in Chicago. For an intense little while, he occupied
all her mind — a good thing, really, in the circumstances. They
even talked about her coming to Chicago on a trial basis. She
didn't mind then that she was sending letter-poems to a poet
(for he was a poet by then, with one book and a lot of little-
magazine publications, but not so famous as now). It was in
the cooler light of rejection that she began to fret about how
really dumb her poems were, and also I think, how they

seemed to have been written by some needy, unfamiliar woman.

So is that it — all the family laundry aired? I feel a perverse desire to say that our cousin Carol Ann was in love with him as well, to sort of spread the blame. But Carol Ann was immune to Roman. She didn't like his two-color eyes or his eccentricities (like wearing a vest he'd made or writing his early poems on paper towels) or his photographing-people-not-wearing-their-neck-brace stories.

I still have a cold shuddery feeling when I think of how he told me, by the fountain downtown, that we had to break up, and of how I cried in public, and worse, of how he said he didn't mean it, we'd stay together, but that was just to shut me up.

But when Markie came, she did not want to talk about all that, although I was ready to get rid of Claudia and Vicky. Manic on the phone, she was now, over coffee, muted and philosophical.

"You know, I thought it would always be all right if I could only get a good partner to crown Our Lady in May, first thing. Did you think that?" she asked me.

"No," I said.

"I did. I thought that in fifth grade. But what good has it done Rosemary Wisnieski? I happen to know that she's a divorced beautician who does dead people's hair, her specialty."

"Does she really?"

"Yes, and it's highly paid. That's what being the hottest May-crowner at Blessed Sacrament leads to: hairdresser to the dead. If only I'd known then, I would have been saved a lot of grief."

Here we had to explain to Claudia and Vicky about the May-crowning ritual itself. Every day in the month of May a pair of us, one boy and one girl, would walk slowly, in a sort of parody of the marriage ceremony, from one end of the classroom to the other where the statue of Mary, the Blessed Virgin, waited. The boy carried a frilled satin pillow with a crown of flowers on it which, when they got there, he offered to the girl. She gravely removed the crown and placed it on the statue's head while the rest of us sang, "O Mary, we crown thee with blossoms today."

"That was it?" asked Claudia, incredulous.

It was. Surely, we said now, there were fertility sort of overtones? There was great significance put on whom one crowned with. Getting a cute guy was very important. The nuns discouraged this, emphasizing the religiosity of the ritual, and how it had nothing to do with things of this world. But those girls who were cute, read sexually desirable, read reproductively fit, got picked first by the best-looking, read highly territorial, read reproductively fit guys. Getting picked first to crown Mary was a sure ticket to teenage pregnancy. Those of us who were late bloomers hung green on the vine until high school or college. I feel that I should be able to explain this to Claudia and Vicky, but they repulse my attempts to give them the big picture, and who knows? — there's probably an evolutionary reason for this.

"My best partner ever was Donald Kovach," I said.

"He used to spit behind the radiator," Markie told Claudia and Vicky. "But didn't you crown with John Thomas Fisher?"

"Well, yes," I said. "But that was because Sister made us pick names out of a hat that year. He probably tried to trade me for someone else." I could remember embarrassingly well how I burned, walking slowly along the aisle next to John, the giggling of my girlfriends, the exquisite touch of his shirtsleeve against my wrist when I took the crown. Would it tilt? Fall off? Would I trip and fall against his actual body?

"There's nobody in my class I'd want to be partners with. They're all disgusting," Vicky said.

"What about Russell?" Claudia said.

"Who's Russell?" Markie and I asked.

"Nobody," said Vicky.

Claudia said that Russell was Vicky's friend Sharon's old boyfriend who Vicky had met at Sharon's birthday party where he had been the only boy. Sharon's mother had taken group pictures of the guests, one with Russell and one without. Now Sharon liked someone else and Vicky had gotten the picture with Russell, where he was only two people away from her and possibly looking in her direction, and stuck it on her mirror. Meanwhile, Vicky yelled, "Shut up shut up shut up shut up," and ran out of the room, taking the bag of cookies with her. Claudia followed her upstairs, where they banged around and slammed doors.

I looked at Markie.

She leaned across and said, "Here's the plan."

I snorted and got up to pour more coffee, but I was interested.

"He's going to stay at the old house with his brother. We can just go over there and see him. We call him up and say how are things, how about talking over old times, etcetera."

"I'd feel stupid."

"He probably reads them," Markie said, lowering her voice

as Claudia and Vicky ran downstairs and then back up. "He gets them out and reads them and laughs. He shows them to his women."

"He doesn't," I said.

"I would if I was him."

"You're a case."

"It's better if we both go. It'll confuse him. Keep him off guard."

"Have you thought of just asking him?"

"Are you crazy?"

But I knew she had thought of it, in fact had probably imagined a whole scene, dialogue, setting, the sun slanting through the venetian blinds, Roman looking at her with renewed interest, thinking how she looked so young (it was true — she did) and perhaps ruefully considering his thinning hair (which he had if he took after his father). I knew she couldn't help it, and I would do the same, had done as a matter of fact ever since she had called me up and the word "Roman" hummed over the wire. It made me mad as hell.

To think about Roman was to be back in a place I didn't want to be anymore. That high school/adolescent thing. Any place is a good place: in the car, in the basement, in the library stacks, in the park up against a tree — you just can't wait to touch, not even sex, although that too, but just to touch. And being in the car with a boy for the first time: the marvelous enclosed feeling. It is like you are in your own little house, you are master and mistress of this small space, adults for the space of a date, capable of movement, action, love.

"I won't do it," I said to Markie.

"All right then," she said. "How about this? We go to the reading and we go up to see him afterward. Perfectly natural. We like poetry, don't we? Old friends going up to say hello, how are you?"

"Hello, how are you, where are my letters?"

"I'll find a way to work it in naturally. Maybe we could go out for a drink or coffee or something."

"Just tell me: why is it so important?"

She made a face at me.

"I mean it."

"Well, it's only partly the letters. I do want them back. I remember bits of them by heart, you know. I'd like to burn them. I'd like to bury them. But it's more than that. I want to see him and sort of repudiate him."

I sat stirring my coffee. I was beginning to feel persuaded. In a way, I would like to see Roman again. I had hardly seen him since he dumped me. When Markie was with him the second time I'd avoided him. What would it be like? I allowed myself to wonder.

"When is it?"

"Aha!" said Markie.

....

"I just took codeine," a woman perfectly unknown to us told Markie and me as we all three stood at the back of the enormous, built-for-the-baby-boom high school auditorium. "I feel a little dizzy."

"What did you take it for?" Markie asked. She was really interested and I bad-mouthed her inwardly for being able to converse with strangers, and not being sick to her stomach like I was.

"Root canal. But I had to come. I used to know him."

"You used to know Roman Mykyta?" I said.

"I worked with him at L & K Insurance. I didn't know him very well. We went out together a couple of times and then he quit."

"When was this?" Markie asked. I could see she was getting ready to set up a timetable.

"I wanted to get a look at the woman who's reading with him. Antoinette whoever. Do you think they've got something going?"

"Antoinette Blumenthal, the poet?" I asked.

"Why not? Poets do it, too. You know how codeine makes me feel? Like I'm floating on a higher plane, like up in the clouds. Does it do that to you?"

"More like I'm in an echo chamber," said Markie.

I said it made me feel kind of muffled in cotton with the pain happening in another room.

The auditorium was filling up. About half of the seats were occupied by boys from the high school who probably had to be there, who probably had to take notes for their English teachers to prove they'd been there, and had paid minimal attention. I could remember how this was. Our school had been an all-girl school and I could easily transpose the sullen graceful jostling boys with their female counterparts, who would be furtively applying lipstick, pulling up socks, passing notes, changing earrings, getting the lowdown on the latest dates, copying homework.

"We ought to sit down," I said.

"Maybe I could sit with you," the codeine woman said. "All these boys make me nervous. I never had children."

We moved down the aisle, slowly. On either side of us

were squadrons of teenage boys, barely under control. Markie
and I were both wearing the same colors — black and blue —
by accident, as we often did. Nothing mystical, just that we
shopped together all the time and had the same taste. We
even had some identical shoes and several skirts that were
impossible to tell apart. We are still in spirit uniform. Why
am I thinking about this? I thought.

We sat down about ten rows from the stage. There were
more adults toward the front, of two types: clerical-looking
men, and women who looked like school mothers; also a few
who surely were nuns or ex-nuns by the look of their hair.
We sat in a row: first Markie (on whose other side was a boy
with a very complicated watch that he was trying to set),
then me, then the codeine woman on the aisle.

The stage was enormous — high, wooden, old-fashioned.
Looking up at it made me feel dizzy. Blumenthal was to read
first, the codeine woman whispered in my ear, a loud hissing
whisper that made the boys around us look in her direction
and smirk. I was glad to hear this. I wanted time.

"Blumenthal is reading first," I said to Markie, using a
deliberately unsingular voice.

"Shut up," she said. "They're starting."

One of the clerical-looking men got up from the first row
and walked to the steps at the side of the stage. This gave me
pause. Was Roman sitting somewhere near? I thought I could
feel his dreadful presence, hardly negated by ten or twenty
feet of hollow space.

The clerical person was talking — "first on our program . . .
great honor . . . whose work has appeared . . ." — who knew
what he was saying? He swung his head sideways several

times while he said these words, as if to check that she was still there, waiting in the wings. And she was. We clapped and she came out. She took her glasses off and put them on several times before she started. Glasses, I thought. Ha.

But I couldn't listen. I was as bad as the boys behind us, who were restive. When we met Roman he was only as old as these boys, as old as the boy with the watch who was now pretending to sleep for the amusement of his friends. He wasn't a poet then, of course, but was just writing poetry in the way that a lot of adolescents and postadolescents do. We — everybody — wrote poems then, especially if we were in love, girls more than boys, but boys sometimes too; it was surefire, if they could manage it.

But these boys — only their bodies were there. There is nothing here, they might have said, only a woman reading, nothing to get hold of, nothing to move, nothing to push into or get out of, only words — death, baby, stone, window, love. They vibrated in their seats, jiggled, bit their nails. At least there were things to laugh at — old people's clothes, the certain way the poet coughed. The color of the carpet was enough to make them die of sat-on laughter, shaking in their seats. Was I upset?

Every poem she read was too long. Every poem she read was one more between me and Roman. I looked over at the codeine woman. She was writing things in a notebook, holding her hand cupped over the page secretively. I imagined Roman backstage — being charming to the stage crew? Sitting pensively with papers in his hands? Peering anxiously into a pocket mirror?

And then it was the last poem; she introduced it that way.

I gripped Markie's hand. The poet read slowly. She thanked us and took her glasses off one final time. We clapped again.

"I don't know. She didn't seem to me like someone Roman would be interested in, do you think?" the codeine woman said to me.

"I don't know," I said. I looked at Markie. She was focused intensely on the right side of the stage. I looked, and behind one layer of curtain saw just the outline, the edge of a body. It was strange to think that up there, out of reach and almost out of sight, was a person I had cried over, who had been my birthday wish on at least two cakes. The clerical man was getting up again. The boys around us were cheering — something to do at last. Roman was coming out on the stage to stand there and grin through his introduction. He was reading his first poem, his very first, he said, written when he was still a student here, maybe written in this very auditorium when he was supposed to be doing something else. I wondered if this was true. It was about driving from the west side of town to the east side to pick up a girl for a date. Who had he dated on the east side?

"He looks just the same," the codeine woman said in my ear.

"He looks so different," Markie said on the other side.

I could hardly see him, he glimmered between then and now, the shine of what he used to be overlaying the middle-aged man. Almost middle-aged. Some things were still the same: a habit of pushing his chin out and up when he said something he wanted to emphasize; the way he stood with feet apart, one hand in his back pocket.

But what did I feel? I felt prickly, as if I had a rash. I felt light-headed, as if my blood had fizzed up like soda.

My mouth was dry, my hands were wet. I didn't think about what Markie was feeling, I'm afraid. I didn't even wonder.

I catechized myself. What had I expected? I answered: (*mea culpa*) I thought he would look at me and be sorry. Instead *I* was sorry. He was only a man, and when we used to know him he was only a boy. By the very evidence of his poems he had had acne, night fears, he had worried about missing the bus, dreamed over unattainable members of the opposite sex.

I relaxed. I really did. And when he announced his final poem, I was almost enjoying myself. It was about his father, he said, or about fathers anyway, about breaking the bonds of mortality or some such, and he leapt into it, reading it like a chant. I sat there, thinking how his poetry had gotten better, and then just listening, and then listening in the intense way that happens sometimes because something is really good. And then at the end, in a final five lines that made the audience draw in its breath, I heard him read about me at the fountain, crying in public, lost in love, cringing under a fatal blow — except it was him, *him* that was sitting on the low wall that surrounded the plumy water, holding *his* hand over *his* face while the lunchtime shoppers and sun seekers passed by. Well.

....

After we took the codeine woman home ("If you're sure it's not out of your way," she said, about fifteen times, but she was having trouble keeping her eyes open), we drove on in silence to my house.

"What'd you think?" I said.

"Oh, I don't know." Markie had gone up afterward and said hello. Me too, actually. She hadn't asked him about the letters. We had all said we should get together next time he was in town. I had shaken his hand.

"Are you coming in?" I asked her.

"I don't know."

"Come on. I'll make cocoa."

Everybody likes cocoa in a different way in our family. Markie likes hers with nutmeg, Claudia with cinnamon, Vicky and me plain. Dak likes his boiled. We had cookies too, gingersnaps from a recipe our grandmother brought over from Europe, and bananas.

"Remember when Aunt Markie ate the green banana and it made her tongue numb?" Claudia said.

"Oh, no." Dak hates it when we do these remembering things.

"Remember when Vicky found the four-leafed clover?" Markie asked. She knows Dak hates this and likes to provoke him.

Claudia made a face. She had never found one. Dak had never found one either, he told her. He picked up his cocoa and left for the basement and his tools. I thought how I would tell him about Roman later, my head against his chest, my hair wound around his fingers.

Markie poured the last of the cocoa into my cup. "You know what it was about Roman?" she said. "It's because he was from before, from then."

She was right, of course. He had the attraction of belonging to our shared past, like the front porch of our old house, or the clothes and makeup we traded, the streetlight we parked under when we came home from dates.

"How old were you when you went out with him, Mom?" Claudia asked.

"Sixteen."

"And she was adorable." Markie banged her spoon for emphasis.

"Well, I'm cuter than you, Mom," Vicky said.

Here is where I wished to make a speech to Claudia and Vicky. I stood up by my chair, looked at the different levels of cocoa in all our cups, enough to make a cocoa musical scale if any of us were skilled enough to play it. "Claudia, Vicky," I planned to say. "What I have to say is very important . . . I implore you . . . Let me tell you what your life will be like . . ." But before I started I paused to think how to word it: how teenage girls must be looked at; how we in our thirties are loath to let go of this feeling of the body as lodestar, magnetized flesh; how life gets made against our desires sometimes, involuntarily; the opposing desires of teenage boys and girls; the ambiguity of a teenage girl's feelings — to protect, to put out.

They waited. "You know, you guys," I said, "your great-grandmother, our grandmother, used beet juice on her mouth when she went to dances in her village in the old country."

"In Austria-Hungary, which got to be Czechoslovakia," said Markie, "but now it's two separate pieces, one Czech and one Slovak," as if she'd been waiting for the opportunity to impart just this set of facts.

"She used it for lipstick, you mean?" Claudia asked. "Gross."

"Well, I am cuter than you. Aren't I?" said Vicky.

I thought she probably was, of course she was, I knew she was, but I didn't know — should I tell her?

BEFORE

::

I got pregnant on my honeymoon. We'd screwed everywhere we could for a year and three months, not using a blessed thing, so I had had this feeling it was a matter of willpower — or not even willpower but just your body knowing that you were ready to settle into life. "O.K.," the message would go from your brain down your backbone — *pow blip kazzam* — right to the ovaries, "it's time RIGHT NOW," and things would release, open up. Your hands would fit themselves to — I don't know, knitting needles, diaper pins — your hair would start to grow itself into your mother's hairstyle, and you'd automatically stop wanting to go out and drink like a fool and dance all night long. I figured this was going to happen when I was around twenty-six; I ought to have had nearly another six years. Oh, I planned to use birth control, I wasn't a total crazy. Just that once though, just for that couple of days, we didn't want to waste time hanging out in a drugstore.

And honestly, we were both embarrassed to go in and buy stuff. Now I slap those tubes of jelly on the counter along

with the Hershey bars and ten-inch fashion doll clothes and
corn plasters, and I don't give a damn. But then I didn't even
like to see the little sign where the contraceptive stuff was
kept that read FEMININE HYGIENE, as if potential babies were
something to be scrubbed away. SPERMICIDE, too — like an
insect spray.

"You go," I'd say.

"No, you," Allen would say.

"I won't."

"You have to go," he'd say. "You promised, Bonnie."

"I did not."

And so on.

The upshot of this ignorance, this bashfulness, was a
baby — or at first not the baby itself, but its symptoms: a
heavy burning ache behind my breastbone, an inability to use
toothpaste, the gradual swelling of my familiar body into a
strange fruit — a gourd or a melon — from which my thin arms
and legs stuck out like twigs.

This brought the relatives around to count backward from
the due date and offer advice. Most Sundays Allen drove me
to one house or another full of aunts, uncles, in-laws, cousins,
family friends. I'd sit in big soft chairs surrounded by people
looking at my stomach and I'd answer questions: "It's due in
April . . . I'm going to work until the last month . . . As long
as it's healthy."

Secretly, I wanted to have a girl. I already had Allen — it
was hard enough learning to live with one male. Besides, I
had it in my mind that I would be able to point out to this
girl baby all the places I had gone wrong and that would be
at least one set of mistakes she wouldn't have to make. When
I rode on the bus to work in downtown Cleveland and looked

out the window at West Twenty-fifth Street, the way I'd
been doing for years, when I washed the dishes, staring at the
yellow kitchen wall in front of me, when I waited in line at
the bank or the supermarket, I'd be thinking of these things
I'd have to tell her. About speaking up for yourself, about
avoiding regret, how to tell if someone is lying, what to say
when it's your fault.

And actually I was sure it would be a girl. I had only sisters,
three of them, and I had the further evidence of my blood
relatives: nine aunts to three uncles. My mother's mother
raised her children by herself after Grandpa left — years of
hard work and no rest, and then some ten years of sitting
back and receiving the fruits of her labor: respect, tiny grandchildren to pet and hand back, meals cooked for her in her
own kitchen by her daughters and daughters-in-law. We are
a family of bossy women, talky women, women who intend
to be taken seriously. So it was natural that from my body,
so like my mother's and my grandmother's, I would produce
another. Allen had nothing of this kind of sexual solidarity
on his side. He had a brother and a sister and no visible aunts
or uncles. What could he say? He tried to get under my skin
by bringing up rumors that twins ran in his family, but I took
this for what it was, pure devilment.

We had an apartment then. What a trip it was, moving
into that apartment. I remember particularly how enamored
I was of a green teapot — leaf green with gold trim. I put it
up on a shelf over the sink and turned on the light nearby to
admire how it looked. That was the center of the apartment
to me, that teapot on that shelf, the picture of what the rest
would be when I fixed it up. It was night by the time we
were moved in and we all sat around and ate pizza — Annie

from work, Allen's brother, John, and his buddy Ted; my best friend from school, Rose, and her sister Ellen; Jimmy Spicer and all that crew. All we had to drink was a six-pack of Champale that someone had brought and put in the refrigerator. No one would admit to having brought it. We poured it into Dixie cups and drank it down, rank and beery-sweet.

Annie and Rose and I went to look at the bedrooms. Not Ellen — she wanted to stay with the guys: what a slut she was then. "This is going to be the baby's bedroom," I said to them. "It's going to be yellow and pink, two walls each color. Curtains with a yellow stripe." My old crib was in there already, scarred and scratched, wood-colored, pictures of lambs and rabbits at the head and foot. Probably we ought to have painted it but I didn't want to cover up the lambs and rabbits — my sisters and I had looked at them when we were too young to know what they were, and traced them with our fingers, and I wanted my girl to do the same, to look at them with her unfocused eyes and pat them with her fat hands.

"Do you have a changing table?" Rose asked me. She didn't know a thing about changing tables and I knew it.

"No, and I don't want one," I said. "I'm going to use the top of the low dresser."

They looked at me, looked at my stomach, and looked away. They were horrified, I knew. I was horrified, too, in a way, by the swell of my stomach and by everything else, but also smug at having done it. Without even trying.

"Are you going to work after?" Annie asked me.

"When it's six months, I'm going back." I was always very careful to say "it." I knew it was a girl but I felt it might jinx things if I said "she" right out. I was afraid that something could shift in my body, a slow turn from one sex to the other.

"I don't think it's right to leave a little baby," Rose said. "Not until they go to school."

I sat down on a box and took my shoes off. "Give it a rest, Rose," I said. I knew she was saying what her mother said. They'd had no thought in their heads of babies, her and Annie. They weren't pregnant. They didn't know what to think of me at all. I leaned back against the wall and arched my spine, stretching, with the curve of my stomach pushed out. They looked at it, and their hands went to their own bodies. Annie put one hand on her own stomach; Rose's fingers fluttered, touching her chest, her hips, twitching at her clothes.

"I'm going to breast-feed," I said.

"God, you're not," Annie said.

"I am, too," I said. "They get bigger if you do." All three of us looked at my chest.

This was bold talk on my part. Sometimes I felt quite different. Sometimes I wanted out of my body. I didn't feel bad, really — that wasn't it. I felt dreamy and sleepy. I sat for hours looking at baby books, reading about pureeing fruit and the order of immunization, sometimes sitting there looking out the window with my hand on the book, sometimes falling asleep with my cheek on the open pages. There was one book in particular that I liked, that said how to manage if you had one baby, then what to do if you had two, then three, then four. How to take four children for a trip on the bus was one of the things in this book. You were supposed to hold one by the hand who was holding another by the hand, one in a collapsible stroller, one in a sling against your chest. There was a picture of this woman wearing a dress and a hat taking money out of her shoulder bag and giving it to the smiling bus driver, with all these round-faced children clustering around her like the angels that frame the margins of holy cards. I loved that book. I got it out of the library three times.

No, I felt fine, really. What worried me was this feeling of inevitability. I was going to have a baby and there was *nothing I could do about it.* I couldn't change my mind, couldn't say, "Wait, time out, I'd like to think about this for a minute." Somewhere in front of me were some solid hours of pain and a baby coming. I was going to grunt and bleed. My body was going to open. It was unbelievable, ridiculous, and yet I had to believe it.

I took the position of suspecting everything that was said to me. What did they know? — "they" being the doctors and my female relatives. They were all so old. They'd been proved wrong already. I was proud that I'd known I was pregnant before the doctor said so, even though the first two tests were negative. They'd said I'd have morning sickness, that I'd swell up with water, but I hadn't.

"What's the doctor doing for me?" I asked Allen. We were in bed and, against my protests, he was rubbing cocoa butter into my stomach, where the skin stretched over the baby. I wanted no special methods or precautions taken.

"What?" he said.

"Not a thing. Not a fucking thing."

He put his hand over my mouth. "Nice language for a mother."

I said I had to say it now, before I had to be a good example. I was feeling cross and cranky. I closed my eyes so as not to have to look at the greasy mound of my belly. I was seven and a half months, and I finally needed maternity clothes: just unbuttoning the fly of my jeans and wearing a long shirt no longer worked. My breasts were bigger already and Allen was showing signs of fascination with them, which I decided to find revolting and depraved.

"You have to go to the doctor," he said reasonably.

I hated him for saying this. "I go there and they make me give them a sample and the nurse weighs me and then I sit around in the waiting room with all these other swollen women and I read *Highlights* and then I go in and he gives me a hard time about gaining too much and asks if I've got any problems and I say no. That's it."

"Umhmm," Allen said. He moved his face against my shoulder, nuzzling from side to side, each sidesweep carrying him a little farther onto my breast.

"Cut it out, Allen. Pay attention."

"Well, they can tell things from those tests, can't they?"

"You don't know anything about it. You don't know a thing." I threw the cocoa butter on the floor and rolled over.

It wasn't that I didn't want sex. Contrary to what the doctor warned, I wanted it just as much as before. And I got plenty of attention too, not only from Allen. I never would have credited it, but there are a lot of men who think it's sexy if you're pregnant. Even at nine months, straining at the seams of those horrible maternity smocks, I'd get whistles when I was walking down the street. Guys would come up to me at parties and make jokes about buns in the oven so as to have an excuse to pat my stomach. Partly it was curiosity, I'm sure. We'd never known anyone that got pregnant before — anyone our age, that is. I was the first in our crowd. Frankly, I looked great. My skin cleared up, for one thing.

So I wanted to do it. Allen wanted to do it. But when we did it, something was wrong. We seemed to be feeling our way, as if we were in a crowded room or a dark empty place; and we knew the other person was there but we couldn't see each other. We kept trying, but it was no good. When we finished we'd hug, we'd turn on the radio and listen to late-night talk shows, and Allen would tell me jokes, and we'd fall asleep laughing. Some things were still O.K.

But I worried about this full stop to the thrilling part of my sex life. Was this what had happened to all those sexless women my mother's age? You got pregnant and some switch in your body turned off all that teenage juice? You turned your cheek and pursed your lips instead of opening your mouth? You put your hands on his chest to push him away instead of to feel his hard little nipples? Watched TV together all evening, not talking, and then slept not touching?

By this time I'd cut my hours at the office to half and all I had to do in the afternoons was sit around and think. How long does it take to do the dishes? I never made the bed. This is on principle: what's the point of making it look unused, unless it's to impress people? I could have baked, but I was big as a house already. I could have watched the soaps. Actually, I did watch them sometimes, but half the actors and all the story lines were different from when I used to watch them in high school and I couldn't pay enough attention to catch up.

So I'd sit in the big armchair in the front room and look out the window and think. And I'd take long slow walks, thinking. Sometimes I thought about our honeymoon. It wasn't much, but it was fine. We went to Chicago, where we had friends we could stay with and save the cost of a motel, except one going and one coming back. With these friends, we went to some ball games and out dancing and hung out on the North Side like we used to when we were all going to school there. At the time I saw my adult life as a wonderful extension of my one year of college: lots of driving around, recreational drinking, freedoms opening out one after another. The last day, we went to the dunes on Lake Michigan with a picnic. We forgot the charcoal, but we were so hungry after swimming that we ate the hot dogs cold, with the warm wind blowing sand at us; grains of sand got between our teeth and made interesting gritty noises when we chewed. We grinned at each other, baring our sandy teeth, and took pictures of our legs all lined up together, our pumped-up biceps, our arms buried from shoulder to wrist in sand, with only the hand sticking out, fingers wiggling. We all hugged each other after and Allen and I drove off, still in our wet bathing suits, and immediately started looking for a motel although it was only five-thirty. Even so, we didn't find one for a long time. I sat as close to Allen as I could and tormented him while he drove, putting my hands inside his shirt and trying to undo his pants. A couple of times we pulled off the road and necked furiously, but we kept on. When we found a motel it was almost seven and we fell on each other, we melted for each other, we opened up all the way. That might have been the time, that one.

A month before my due date, supposedly spring, the weather was still gray, dripping, sleeting. I wasn't reading baby books anymore. All I had in front of me, between me and the baby, were a couple of "surprise" showers — one for relatives, one for girlfriends. My mother had told me about them so I wouldn't turn up wearing something ratty. That was too bad. A surprise would have been distracting, at least — twenty dressed-up women hiding in closets and behind the living-room suite, jumping out. I sat around and felt sorry for myself for not having a surprise in my future.

Annie, Ellen, and Rose came over sometimes. I'd known them all since grade school and they should have been a comfort. But I seemed to be looking at them from a long way off, across the great expanse of my stomach. I was so tired of it all, too tired to lift my hand or shake my head no when Annie brought me a cup of stinking herb tea. They sat and chattered around me about a whole fun world that was no longer open to me.

I couldn't shop, couldn't bear to look at myself in a mirror. When I undressed at night I kept my eyes on a level so as not to see what was going on under my chin. Bad enough to see it with clothes over it. Going out for drinks after work: "drinks," "work" — words no longer in my vocabulary. Sex, men, flirting — ha. I wasn't a member of any sex anymore. I was a husk, a pod — a container, ready to split open.

I kept thinking and dreaming then of things coming open — of seams splitting, of cartons breaking and spilling their contents, of volcanoes, and, more horribly, of wounds, awful gashes that oozed unlikely substances: peanut butter, mud, ketchup. Sometimes it was melons slashed by a knife, all the seeds visible and gleaming wet. I could hardly stand to look at food just then, but I ate constantly, I just shoveled it in. Allen would watch me eat for another fifteen minutes after he'd finished — horrified, I think, to see all this stuff going in, maybe thinking I was going to explode, or give birth right there in front of him.

Allen was far away from me, too. Hugging was so ridiculous

that I wouldn't let him do it. Kissing was out of the question, real kissing. To really kiss you have to wrap your arms around each other — neck, waist, wherever. You have to press up against each other, feel every part of his body pushing into or surrounding every part of yours. We lay in bed next to each other every night, holding hands, staring up at the ceiling until we fell asleep.

I stopped even thinking about the future. All there was, was now. There was my body with another body pushing around in it. I couldn't remember what my stomach or my breasts had looked like before. I could hardly focus on the baby as any real thing. When Allen wanted to talk about names I really didn't care, but I made myself take a stand, on principle. There was no problem with a boy's name: Allen, for Allen; Joseph, for my father. We agreed about this, and, anyway, I still knew it would be a girl, and a girl had to be named this name I'd been carrying around since I was a kid, the name I'd wanted for myself instead of Bonnie: Rachel. It was not a silly name, not a name that could sprout a dopey nickname. It had a wonderful sound in your mouth. It was even biblical. But Allen wanted to name a girl after his sister. Debbie — I ask you. This is what we talked about those last weeks, constantly — at breakfast, at dinner, in bed. There was no compromise available, it seemed. We both hated all the other family names on both sides. We made lists. We read out loud from the *Best Baby Book of Names*. It kept our minds off other things, like the fact that we were not allowed to screw anymore, even if we'd wanted to.

On a Saturday exactly two weeks before my due date, my mother-in-law drove over. Why? Who knows? Just to give us a hard time, is what I thought then. She came in and asked

a lot of questions and poked around all over the apartment.
Did I have my suitcase packed? Had I cooked up a lot of stuff
and put it in the freezer for Allen while I was in the hospital?
Did I have a diaper service yet? The answer to all these
questions was "No." I could hardly bring myself to think
about what was going to happen. I'd been telling myself there
was plenty of time. It was just like when I was in school and
there was this big paper due that I had to do a lot of library
research for, or I would have to make a clay relief model of
South America with tiny products and resources glued to it.
I would always start out with big plans, make lists, imagine
the comprehensiveness of what it would be like when it was
finished — the detail, the papier-mâché bananas, the small
clay figures with miniature serapes. But I would put it off and
put it off until there were only three days left, and then I'd
panic for one day and rush around for another and stay up
until two in the morning on the third, my mother hovering
anxiously over me as I grimly glued and pinned. So now the
suitcase lay open and empty in our bedroom. The list of
diaper services lay beside the telephone, unused. I had no
intention of freezing up big batches of lasagna or whatever.

"Allen wants to eat out while I'm gone," I said to my
mother-in-law.

She was upset by this, I could see, but she had the good
sense not to say anything.

In order to get out of the apartment we went and got in
the car and drove to the park near where we lived. It was real
spring now, April, and actually warm. The sun was shining
weakly. We parked and walked decorously down the path,
the three of us. To our right there was a field with people
playing catch and Frisbee, and some swings with children on

them, swinging in great arcs, pointing their toes toward the sky. To our left there was the creek, and what Allen and I called the mountain. It was only a small hill, red clay and crumbling fast on its steep sides. But trees grew on it and there was a path on one side that you could scramble up to get to the top, which was a narrow ridge. Allen and I had often climbed it when we first lived in the apartment.

My mother-in-law was fussing with her purse as we walked. Allen had his hands in his pockets. He was scuffing up bits of leaves and gravel with the toes of his tennis shoes, walking his lively, good-natured walk. Even my mother-in-law, with her arthritic knees, was bouncing along. I felt like a sack of cement on stilts. What I wanted to do was climb the hill.

"Let's go up," I said to Allen.

"Don't be silly." My mother-in-law frowned.

"Come on, Allen," I said.

"You can't climb up there with that stomach." My mother-in-law was showing alarm and I meanly enjoyed it.

"We can just go part way," I said to Allen, but I meant to go all the way once I got him up there.

He looked doubtful, but he followed me to the place where you have to step over the narrow arm of the creek that circles the hill. I stepped across, and stood waiting for him on the other side.

"Bonnie! Bonnie!" my mother-in-law called from the path. She was holding her purse in front of her with both hands.

"I'm going to do it!" I shouted to her.

We started up. The parts that were easy before were harder. The bits of the path where you had to plant your feet carefully because the ground sloped away were terrible. My balance was different. I felt like a tightrope walker, holding

my arms out to keep upright. My stomach got in the way
whenever I had to climb over the exposed roots of the trees,
as if I was mounting a staircase. I had to scrabble up sideways
and couldn't use my hands as much as I'd have liked. Finally
we came to the part of the path that was like a chute, that
you had to climb duck-footed, setting your feet at a careful
angle, bending forward and rushing up, to gain momentum.
I did all this. Allen was just behind me. I made it up to the
bend in the chute. I fell to my hands and knees.

"Bonnie! Bonnie!" my mother-in-law was yelling, and I
could hear Allen gasping.

"You dope, you jerk, you bitch," he said. He gripped me
by my hips and shook them, put his arms around me and
pushed his face into the small of my back.

I let my arms relax until I was lying on my side, my face
against the red crumbly clay, which was cool and slightly slick
under my cheek. Looking up, I could see the top just above
us, another ten feet — the hard ridge of the hill that I knew
was bare of grass but carpeted with pine needles that slid
pleasantly under your feet. When you stood up at the top
and looked down, the eroded sides, rawer and redder than
the hard-packed soil of the ridge, sloped away from under
your feet and you felt as if, with very little effort, you might
slide down them into the water of the creek. Just one step,
one small movement; no thought was necessary.

Allen was crying a little, which I thought was very sweet
of him. "Oh, I'm all right," I said. I sat up so I could take his
hand and kiss the palm. My mother-in-law was hesitating at
the brink of the stepping-over place, holding her purse up
almost over her head.

"I'm not going to do it!" I yelled to her.

"What?" she yelled back.

"I won't do it!" I yelled.

Allen and I started down. I slid over the bad places on my butt, Allen going first to stop me if I fell. When we got to the bottom our clothes were dusty and smeared with red. My mother-in-law looked at us as if we were accident victims. "You'll be in the hospital before morning after that," she said. I didn't care.

She was right, though. In the car on the way back I felt the first tightenings and loosenings, not yet pain. And after she'd gone home, I started to have mild contractions, and then a major one — the big pain rippling down, pushing my thoughts down, locating my center lower and lower. All the things I didn't know — when to start solid food, about Montessori, how to satisfy the sucking reflex — they didn't bother me a bit then, while I was in the car going to the hospital with Allen. It was like riding a comet or a roller coaster, this intense purposeful movement after all those months of waiting. I didn't see anything ahead of me — not our lovely daughter; not the tired doctors who would talk to Allen afterward, my blood on their hands and their clothes; not my flattened, empty stomach; not my sallow face in the mirror the first time I could get up by myself and go to the bathroom; not Allen with a mask on his face bringing the baby through the door for me, my lips saying "Rachel" for the first time. I didn't see any of that. But I could feel events rushing toward me as they wheeled me in, I could feel my life changing, the old familiar parts of it crumbling away and a new shape emerging that I would come to know, and God, I was so excited I could hardly stand it.

WE

::

We all got married — Suzanne, and Virginia, and I — and it was all we ever wanted to be at the time. I fought with my parents to get married, and Suzanne ran away from home with her boyfriend to get married, and Virginia saved her money for a year and eight months, eating a bag lunch at work every day and walking up from the square to save the five cents for the transfer and making her own clothes and only seeing movies when they came to the drive-in — all to get married.

And then we had done it and we were married. Sex all the time. Our own houses (rented). A whole list of things that would not have been gathered together except for us: toasters, glassware, unbreakable dinner sets with a rim of gold around the white plates, towels we were going to paint the bathroom to match. It was heaven. Every day we woke up to different clock radios all set to the same rock station and we had breakfast with our husbands, except for Suzanne who said good-bye to hers at 2:30 A.M. unless he tried very hard not to wake her and only kissed her on the forehead before he left. Then maybe we did the dishes or made the bed or put something out for dinner. I would get this really happy feeling when I was putting on my coat if I could look around and everything was nice: the glasses turned upside down and shining, the carpet speckless and smooth like a mowed lawn, the pillows on the bed fat and undented. Or maybe we only had time to put on eyeliner and go. We went to work and at lunch (still a bag lunch for Virginia, because of saving for their future house) we told stories about our husbands. Then we went home and a) fixed dinner from a new recipe, or b) called out for pizza, or c) went to a sit-down restaurant that wasn't too expensive. Later at home, we watched TV with our husbands, with our arms around each other, or somebody would come over and we'd play gin rummy or pinochle with the tape player turned up loud. We could have done anything we wanted to do, that was the thing.

And then (we still didn't know each other yet, although Suzanne lived only one house away from me) we'd been married for a while and there was something funny about it. I didn't want to have sex every night, for instance. This was awful, after how it had been. Sometimes I wanted to watch the end of a movie or one of my favorite shows instead of having sex. I didn't tell him, but I felt sick. Then I got used to it. Suzanne says it was the other way for her: she could tell sometimes he wanted to listen to the ball game on the radio instead. Virginia didn't say much about this, but she's shyer than Suzanne and me. And also when he and I were at home together, alone, one of us would always be calling up someone to come over. He would call up his buddies to come over and work on the car. Or I would call up my sister and

her husband to come over and watch a movie. I had a feeling
like — "What's next?"

Right here was when I met Suzanne, in the supermarket.
I'd seen her around a lot before, in the yard or driving up
her driveway in her car or hanging up bedspreads on the
clothesline in her backyard, so I thought what the hell and I
said hello. The thing is I probably wouldn't have said hello
earlier on because then I had everything I wanted. But on this
day — it was April — there was a wind scooting little pieces of
paper around the supermarket parking lot and a feeling in
the air like you should be driving fast someplace and I didn't
know it but I was pregnant. I wanted something and Suzanne
looked like she had some of what I wanted. She was wearing
a new miniskirt and mirror shades, and she had a way of
walking as if she was in a commercial. She was pregnant, too,
but she already knew and had gone right from the doctor's
to buy the miniskirt so she could wear it for a couple of
months before her stomach pushed out.

But whatever we thought we wanted or thought each other
was like didn't matter — was forgotten, even — because from
the first words we said to each other we knew we were going
to be friends. I had thought that wouldn't happen anymore
now that I was married. I went back from the supermarket
to her house for coffee (I felt like my mother — having coffee
and doughnuts with a neighbor) and we talked for two hours
while my groceries melted and slumped in the car. I can't
remember what we talked about. Everything. Suzanne said
it was like being in love, which I found upsetting when she
said it. But it was true. We leaned across the table toward
each other, that morning and other mornings, drinking cups

of coffee (later Sanka) and eating and smoking until we had to quit, and told each other stories about our pasts, our families, our school loves, our hopes for adventure. It wasn't like a conversation, which sounds too stiff and polite; it was more like a piece of music where we each had parts that overlapped, or a play when the actors say what is closest to their hearts.

And then, when we were about five months along, Virginia and her husband moved into the house on the other side of Suzanne. If Suzanne and I hadn't gotten to be good friends so fast, things might have been difficult or different. There might have been jealousy or misunderstandings or whatever. But as it was we knew each other so well already that there was room for Virginia, who was nice and really not a demanding sort anyway. She wasn't pregnant but was planning to be, and in two months she was.

For a while we didn't have to worry about the thing of being married. For quite a long while. There was all the business of doctor visits, baby showers, maternity clothes, painting the extra bedroom. And then the hospital, the drive home with the baby looking so cute in the infant seat for the first time, the adoring grandparents waiting at home with giant panda bears and potty seats that played tunes. And then the long plunge into babyness. All of life was baby life: baby food, baby clothes, baby wipes, the baby-changing table, baby's schedule, baby's nap, baby's bad time with breast-feeding/colic/teething. All our stories were baby stories: how baby had thrown up yellow, how baby had pulled the pierced earrings right out of our ears, how baby had rolled over for the first time while we were out of the room and almost fallen off the bed, how baby would not go to sleep until a certain song was played on the tape player.

Suzanne and I both had two, Virginia only one: she seemed shy and not very definite, but she was a planner. And for three years, we were submerged together. We woke up at seven and sank into our lives, making breakfast/lunch/dinner, cutting food up into bird bites, taking slow walks pushing strollers or with a staggering child hanging on to our hands, slipping the top diaper off towering stacks of whiteness, pulling out the potty chair, holding someone else's eager flesh in our arms, holding it back from destruction by fire, cars, household pets, electric sockets. Our husbands visited every day, between work and going out and going to bed, but we scarcely noticed. And every night we went to bed later than we wanted and as soon as we touched the sheets we found ourselves rising up into sleep and dreams, as light as birds.

And then there was a change. At first we thought it was just because Virginia had gone back to work. Her little girl was three and old enough for day care, she said. We were amazed that she had had the strength to think ahead — she had been on the school's waiting list for months. She went back to the phone company — not to her old job, but to a new one they found for her. This made Suzanne and me discontented. Our younger children were only one and a half and two — too young, we thought, for day care. And we had no jobs to go back to. Suzanne had gone to college for a while, but she had quit when her money ran out and her family refused to lend her any. Come back home and get married was not what they said, but they might as well have. I had never been to college at all. Virginia, though, had her

B.A. For a while we couldn't like her as well as we had, and we looked for signs that her little girl was suffering from going to day care. Was she thin? Was she more quarrelsome and whiny? Was a career more important, Suzanne and I asked ourselves, than your child's happiness? Could you have a career at the phone company?

We got together more and more often to discuss this, and then other things. We were surprised to find ourselves thinking again, it had been so long. And then we realized that the change was in the kids, too, and that that change had made it possible for us to think, to put our heads above water, to begin to float again on the surface of the world. They, the kids, were becoming people, sometimes responsible for themselves, capable of wishes that were not dictated or instigated by us, wanting to be on their own. The older kids had been like this for a while but we hadn't noticed.

And we noticed other things, too: that our husbands were still there, but that things between us were not quite the same. That we were not as young as we still thought of ourselves as being. That we looked different — older, or maybe just not taken care of. It's a wonder we didn't lynch Virginia for only having had one and being already out in the world. Suzanne and I knew that we would have to wait — did we ever discuss this? — until the little kids were older. It would be at least a year, but probably more like two. We couldn't afford Virginia's day care, so it would have to be the church day/play, where they only took four-year-olds. But what to do in the meantime, now that we were conscious again?

You might have thought we would have taken another look at our husbands. But things with them had gotten into a different way, and maybe we thought that was the way it was supposed to be, or maybe we thought it would do no good to try and change. We had things we did with our husbands on the weekends, and we went out sometimes, but really we had separate lives. I had a memory of how I thought before we got married that we would spend all our time together, that we would go places together and do things as ordinary as shopping for the fun of it, but now I knew how dumb that was. We didn't think of getting divorced; we knew we were married, and that was that. But the feeling from the day in April came back, worse than ever, and Suzanne and I put our heads together to do something about it. But it was hard to even think of change when things had been the same for so long.

Oh, we were so bored. Nothing ever happened on our street, except the regular visits of the mailmen and the meter men and the teenagers who stuck flyers into our mailboxes or rubber-banded them to the banisters of the porch. Nothing happened at the supermarket except that you heard from the cashiers about who had died in the neighborhood. Nothing happened at church except you could see who had new clothes or was pregnant. But we were determined to look for what there was.

The first thing we tried was new recipes. For a while we cooked something new every day. We got cookbooks out of the library — Hawaiian cookbooks, make-your-own-bread cookbooks, tomato cookbooks, dinner-in-an-hour cookbooks. We bugged our aunts and grandmothers for family recipes which we wrote out and exchanged on file cards. At every dinner we tried them on our husbands and children. Every morning when we had coffee, instead of buying doughnuts from Snow White the way we used to, one of us made something: chocolate-chip kuchen, apricot-sour-cream coffee cake, banana-bran muffins with lemon glaze. Instead of Oreos and chips, our kids ate snacks of prune-peanut crunch, sesame bread sticks, carrot-and-cheese-cubes on a stick. We made ice cubes with single grapes and cherries frozen inside, we candied violets in the spring and rose petals in the summer. We had gala dinners to which our husbands and children — and Virginia and her husband and child — came, uncomfortable and surprised to find themselves all together in one house or the other. But that was no good, and it was back to meatloaf and macaroni and cheese.

Next: sewing. I had a sewing machine that I had hardly ever used, bought from a high-pressure salesman in the first months of our marriage. My husband and I were so dumb, and the salesman was so powerful and certain. We sat before him on the couch holding each other's hands behind a cushion and we said yes to everything, yes to the cross-stitching attachment, yes to the five-year service contract. The sewing machine sat in the hall between the bedrooms, sometimes with things stacked on it, sometimes used as a stool by one of the kids. But we dragged it out, Suzanne and I, and we got a pattern that was marked "Easy-Sew" and we picked out cloth at the Sewtex fabric store, with the kids rampaging up and down the aisles and begging for cards of buttons and long curling strips of ribbons and lace. We looked at but prudently did not buy the patterns for baby and children's clothes — little rompers with duck appliqués, little dresses with ruffled sleeves and hems. We planned how we might make all our clothes except for coats and bathing suits and underwear. The cloth was wonderful to carry home, heavy and bright-colored, smooth to touch, folding over and over on itself without wrinkling. Mine was golden, yellow and full of light. Suzanne's was silver, a gray as pale and shining as the moon.

And all that month we pinned the thin crumpled tissues of the pattern to the cloth with sharp, glittery pins and flashed the metal of the scissors through the folded layers and attached the pieces to each other under the whir of the machine's needle. They were simple dresses: a panel for the front and one for the back, attached at the shoulders by slender strips of cloth that were meant to be tied in a bow. But we sweated and swore over them, sewed pieces backward, stabbed our fingers with pins until they bled. The kids ate cookies and pickles and M & Ms and Popsicles unheeded for the last two days before we were done. We tried the dresses on in Suzanne's bedroom, pulling the shades in the middle of the day and standing on her bed unsteadily, laughing and holding on to each other, to see if they looked good in the back. The ties tied, we exclaimed to each other. They were real dresses, wearable, that we could go out in and no one would be able to tell that we had bled on them. But never again, I said, and Suzanne agreed — never again would I sew another thing except for putting on a button or turning up a hem.

And then we joined a book club. Once a month the members met to discuss a book that had been agreed on beforehand. Suzanne and I were conscious that we had not used our minds much for a while. We went to the library and got out the book, a very long novel by a famous South American writer, and read it in tandem, borrowing it back and forth. What do you think it means, I would ask Suzanne between loads of laundry, when that old guy comes back and looks just the same but he should have been dead for a hundred years? How about that blood? she asked me when we were giving the kids peanut-butter sandwiches for lunch, letting them spread their own so they would learn to be independent even though it took so long and was so hard to clean up. What did you think when that blood dripped and flowed like a stream down the street to the house of the murdered man's mother? We didn't know. We went to the meeting, held at a member's house, and sat waiting for enlightenment, but no one asked the questions we were interested in, and we were afraid to ask them. The other members were teachers, mostly, and they argued with one another and harangued and pounded the arms of their chairs and were so terrifying to Suzanne and me that we could hardly eat the pasta salad and brownies afterward. Did we have suggestions for the next book? one of the teachers asked us nicely when we sat balancing our plates and glasses. We said no.

It was summer again now: longer nights, warm sweet air. It seemed like a long time since we had had any fun. In the mornings we sat drinking countless cups of coffee while the kids drove up the driveway and down the driveway on their Big Wheels. We sat on Suzanne's back steps watching the kids play with dirt and water under the apple trees. We lay on a blanket in my backyard while Suzanne's husband mowed the lawn. And we moaned, and we moped. Why didn't we see any fun people anymore? Why didn't we ever get to go anyplace? Why didn't anyone we knew have a party? Why didn't we? It would be an outdoor party, we planned, with lights in the trees and a speaker hooked up outside. While the kids threw sand at each other we made a guest list, a food list, a decorations list, a music list. Twenty times we decided

what to wear, and twenty times we changed our minds. On
the night of the party, we carted the kids off to Grandma's,
harried our husbands to do the electrical and musical prepara-
tions. We combed the silken lengths of each other's hair,
applied layers of scarlet and heather and ivory bisque to the
smooth skin of our faces. "You look wonderful," we said to
each other.

Virginia came early with a goose-liver pâté and her husband. How is work? we said. She told us about the feud
between her supervisor and the most senior operator, about
the new system being installed that would require them to
learn a new form of data entry, about the new coffee machine
that she and her coworkers had chipped in to buy. She said
that she was thinking of getting her own car and had found
three new places to eat lunch and wanted to update her
wardrobe to a more office look. What's new? she asked us.
We looked at each other, and then away. Our kids had new
teeth, new scrapes and bruises, new words learned from illicit
television and unapproved friends. Suzanne had new eye
shadow. I had just gotten a new bra and had found a more
efficient way to pack the freezer. Nothing much, we said.

And then we set out to have fun. Fun was drinking new
combinations of liquor and mix, drinking out of other people's glasses, perching on the arms of chairs and saying outra-
geous things, letting someone light our cigarette and looking
into his eyes with the flame between us, talking about things
that our mothers would have been shocked to hear said aloud,
playing the music as loud as possible but not so loud that the
neighbors would call the police. It was fun to sing along with
the music from where we lay in the grass under the rocking,
bobbing lanterns that hung in the apple trees, and to race

back and forth between our two houses for more drinks, more cookies, more celery stuffed with peanut butter. We were glad to go to the store for more ginger ale, recruiting someone to go with us who was not our husband, walking down the street in the welcome dark and into the dead daylight of the streetlights. We though it might make us finally and forever happy to kiss someone in the kitchen, leaning against the sink, one hand on the cool smooth curve of the enamel and the other touching the weave of a shirt that we had never washed or ironed or sewed a button on. The morning after the party, though, was just the same, filled with cornflakes and daytime television, and there were the dirty glasses and erupting ashtrays as well.

We took a class in calligraphy. We made a list of places to take the kids and we took them there: fast-food lunches, swimming, the park with the jungle gym or the park with the hiking trails, for walks, to story hour. We took up badminton and played for weeks with anyone who showed up on a court marked on my lawn with white spray paint, waiting our turn lounging on the old car that my husband thought he might get around to fixing someday, our backs against the front window, legs stretched out on the metal of the hood, heads thrown back to the sky. We played on into the dark, until we could see nothing except the small white blur of the shuttlecock arcing across the yard, and then not even that, so that we struck out at it on faith.

It was fall. And then maybe, we thought, if we go out together? . . . Just the girls, since our husbands didn't want to go anyway. We could go to movies, to plays, to dinner. We went out with an old friend of mine, still unmarried, whom we envied and felt superior to. It was more fun to go

out with Janine because she was single and we were not and
we could do anything because we were not involved in the
game the way she was. You guys, she would say, I can't
believe you guys. Will you cut it out? she would say. We
went to dinner and ate unfamiliar foods, spicy and fragrant.
We went to plays and strained forward in our seats the better
to enter another world. We went to a Tupperware party
when we were high as kites. We went to bars where we met
podiatry students who claimed to be amazed when we said
how old we were and some of whom got sentimental and
clingy when it was time to leave. But when we went out, no
matter how immensely silly we became, or how high we got,
no matter how many places we went and how late we stayed
out, drinking cup after cup of coffee at an all-night restaurant
while we talked and talked about our lives and how they
disappointed and how they might gladden us, when we went
back it was still the same.

And then I got the flu, a long, lingering flu. I was sick as a
dog — so sick that my husband had to do for the kids, get
their dinners and take them in and out of the bathtub and
read them the same book over and over again. And Suzanne
was invited to join her cousin's bowling team while I was
sick. Twice a week I watched her from my front window,
where I was lying on the couch using up Kleenex as she got
picked up by a carful of women wearing satin team jackets.
And when I was well she came over and told me she'd stayed
after one night and made out with the bartender. I thought
I'd never get over it.

So what happened? Nothing really. Everything went on a
little while longer, until we got to the end of this period in
our lives, until we stopped looking for something that we

didn't have or know. But we didn't stop because of despair, or because we were tired of looking, but because it was time. Suzanne got a job at an office. I started college. We started meeting Virginia downtown for lunch. We threw our jeans and T-shirts to the back of the closet and bought new clothes: suits and blouses for Suzanne, slacks and sweaters and a denim jacket for me. There was new stuff on our minds: day care, time-saving appliances, comfortable yet attractively businesslike shoes, notebooks for shorthand and for notes on Dutch medieval art. And we were still married. We had never been able to forget completely about being married, so our husbands were still there. They still came home and called up their friends to work on their cars and didn't want to go anyplace, but it didn't matter so much anymore. We smiled at them over breakfast and bragged about them at lunch and at night; we thought about sex again, and did something about it. Janine got married and we all went to the wedding and we cried, every one of us — even Virginia, who had just met her.

Now we're too busy to think or to remember the time when Suzanne and I sat in one of our kitchens with the kids milling around while we talked on, oblivious, or cooked together, or sat under the apple trees, of how we were pulled together like magnets every morning after our husbands went to work; how we spent the whole day together; how our kids had lunch together, took naps and went to the bathroom together.

Which is O.K. But do we miss it, what we had together when there was no one else in the world but mothers and children? And do we miss it, the soft solid feel of our children's bodies under our hands, the sweet smell of their breath, their voices in our ears singing the alphabet and the names of trees, puddings, television characters; the look of their bodies asleep, arms and legs flung out like a star or wound in a tight breathing ball; their questions asking why and what and how the world is made and ordered and laid out before us? No. Not every day.

INTERVIEW WITH
MY MOTHER

::

My mother says she sees the ceiling opening like a door. I look up and see the smooth white plaster, no holes, not a crack even. Really, I wish I could see it. Perhaps it is the drugs; if it is, I might sneak the pills in the Dixie cup that the nurse brings and then I will see what she is seeing.

She is in the hospital. She is lying, flat and pale, on the bed and she is hallucinating. But she is not going to die, this is why I can afford to be curious and interested in the possible behavior of the ceiling. Her hair is uncombed, but it often is, that's no reason to feel upset. She has always forgotten to comb it, she always combs it with her fingers, but now she can't bring her arms up to her head with any ease.

The windowpane is rippling, she says.

Yes? I say.

But that's all she wants to say about the other world she can see. So, no, it's only her back, a crushed vertebra. There will be a back brace, exercises, she will refuse the pain pills, take only aspirin, I can see all this ahead of time.

Q: Mother, have you been taking your pain pills?

A: Really, I feel much better. I have them though, if I need them.

In the hospital she is fenced off from me with nurses, doctors, the rails of her bed, the drugs. When we go home I will have her to myself, I think, but what I mean by this I'm not sure.

I guess that what I mean is that I will be able to question her, and now that she is old, before she dies, find out from her — something, I don't know what. It is a sort of construction, a blueprint, a model, something with answers, something logical. It is not the key to family scandals I'm looking for — who slept with whom, who was abandoned, who lied, who was greedy. There is no hidden will, no lost fortune. (Once, years ago, I sat at a frat party and heard my cousin tell a boy we had just met that our grandfather's family had had estates in Scotland but that he had given up his claim when he came to America — a total and complete lie.) Of course, if my mother told me the location to a gold mine or about a secret room where a touch on a panel would reveal to me the hiding place of a big fat diamond — well, that would be nice. But there is no place in her little suburban house for that kind of thing.

No, the treasure I want is in her head, and from time to time I resist an urge to tap her skull with careful knuckles, looking for what's inside, the exact location of memory, of knowledge. When she's heavily asleep from drugs I place my hand on her forehead and let it rest there, waiting for something to rise through the bone to my palm.

Some things I know already, for she has told us, my sister and me, lots of stories. Instead of fairy tales for bedtime, she told us about things that happened when she was young, wild exploits with her nine brothers and sisters. Mysterious old-fashioned objects and concepts appeared in these stories: mustard plasters, pitchforks, overturning outhouses at Halloween, outwitting the truant officer, taking in boarders, butter churns, one-room schools. The houses that she lived in — there were many of them, and she described them all — were more wonderful to us than palaces.

It is not exactly that I want more of these stories, though that would be fine, too. What I want is the key to them. I want to know what she was thinking. I want something to take with me into what lies ahead, for I am forty, I might as well say, forty years old, still someone's child, still looking for direction.

Q: Mother, what did you think when your father went away and came back, and again went away and came back?

It is hard to imagine what she would say to this.

Q: How did you feel, Mother, when he left for the last time?

The stories about their father illustrate things like his temper, his dislike of authority, his love of change. He had itchy feet, she says. If he hadn't, they might have lived forever in Castle Shannon, Pennsylvania, where he ran the only general store around, where they lived in a big old house with an enormous spiraling staircase, a house so big that their mother took in boarders, all single gentlemen.

Some of the stories about her father were our favorites, the story of how our Uncle Charley learned to swim, for instance. Their mother and father were gone for the day and the boys (hard to think of our old uncles, Jim, Charley, Joseph, as "the boys") took advantage of their absence to ride the old sow, as big as a sofa. And when their father came back and caught them, he took out after them — he had a redhead's temper, she would say — and all the boys ran away. The pond was in their path, and they all jumped into it and swam across, even Charley, who up until that time hadn't been able to swim a stroke.

Q: Were you afraid of him? Did you hate him sometimes?

These are the tough ones. I'll have to save these, work up to them.

She is smoothing the starchy sheet with her hand, over and over; this, too, is something she does at home. When we sit at the table after dinner on Sunday, the conversation will turn sometimes to more serious things — someone's cancer, someone's unhappiness, someone's death — and she will touch the tablecloth in just this way, smoothing the wrinkles, making a flat clear place. I don't think she knows that she does this. But we don't end with those sadnesses on Sundays. The talk always turns to what was funny.

I know that my mother and my aunts and their friends were always laughing. I watched them laughing over bridge, my mother holding a Kleenex to her eyes to catch the tears that she laughed out, my aunts, Betty and May, putting down their cards to pound each other on the back. Mrs. Metzner from across the street laughed behind the fan of cards that she held before her mouth, while Mrs. Mangan from next door waved her hand in the air in front of her while she guffawed, holding off further jokes until she had recovered. It was hard for me to understand how adults could be having that much fun.

One of my mother's favorite stories was about laughing, from when she was training as an operator at the telephone company. She had been one of a large class of girls in their late teens learning the long-distance codes — BY for "busy," LD for "long distance," and so on — and something about these two-letter codes struck her as so funny that she started to giggle. She tried to stifle it in her hand, but every new two-letter code struck her as freshly ridiculous, and it was worse when the trainer started them repeating the phrases over and over — "BY busy, BY busy, BY busy" — all these carefully dressed girls anxious to make a good impression, singing out like a chorus, and not even the fact that this was the Depression and jobs were scarce could keep her from laughing right out loud.

Another story was how she and Aunt Elizabeth and Anna and Winnie (Mrs. Metzner and Mangan to me) had gone to the opera. (When she began this story Aunt May always said, "Oh and I didn't go and I missed it all.") The opera was *Tristan und Isolde* — "very romantic, very tragic," my Aunt Elizabeth would always say. They were all dressed in their best — gloves, hats, Mother wearing her blue lace that she still has enshrined in a plastic bag in her closet (to my disappointment I grew too large for it before I was eleven). They were prepared to be ravaged by emotion, amply supplied with handkerchiefs. But the tenor, "a famous man," Mrs. Metzner would always say, was so fat, not at all romantic. And worse, at one point, he began a scene on a sort of divan, and as it went on he kept heaving himself up off the divan and singing a bit and then plopping back down so that a cloud of dust would poof up around him. They couldn't stop laughing even though people were shushing them and giving them dirty looks, because he kept doing it over and over. They had to put their heads between their knees, finally had to leave and gasp out the end of it in the powder room on a pale-green Empire sofa while the attendant looked on, hands in her lap, transfixed.

Q: Weren't you ever upset? Didn't the Depression ever depress you?

I know what she would say to this:

A: We all did our best. We all gave Mom our wages and only saved out some for an allowance. We had a lot of fun, you could have fun without money then.

And she tells stories about how they had fun without money, parties that went on until breakfast, their mother, my grandmother making pots and pots of strong coffee to send the stragglers home. We saved our money, she says, and went to Cedar Point Amusement Park on a boat, dancing all the way. But these stories don't have the bite and excitement of the tales where there is conflict and violence: of how she and her brothers and sisters fought off a gang of neighborhood toughs from the bandstand in Lincoln Park, or of how Aunt Elizabeth was stolen by the Gypsies.

This last was a story that had a powerful hold on me, the story of a little girl who is lost, how they searched everywhere for her, how she was thought to be gone forever, stolen by the Gypsies, how they had almost given her up, and then how she was found by one of the boarders, sleeping at the foot of a seven-foot stalk of corn in the middle of the cornfield, as if it were a city and she asleep on a street, and the stalks skyscrapers so tall to her at three that she might have been in a different country.

It seems so useless that they found her safe, that she had

not been abducted or murdered, because now she is dead. It seems irrelevant that in the meantime, sixty some years, she got married, had six children, had jobs she liked, had a nickname — Betty — dyed her hair blond. I don't know what to do with this information. It seems only fair that everyone know these things. But useless. Perhaps it should only be given out on a need-to-know basis. She was saved. And she died.

I pour myself a glass of water from the plastic pitcher by my mother's bed, flat water, tasteless. She is sleeping now, her hands folded over her stomach, freckled, wrinkled — alive. Once, on my way home from Arizona, I escaped possible death in a car explosion. I have a souvenir from this occasion, a mass of metal like a small sculpture or paperweight that is the melted accumulation of the coins that were in my purse that day. So — do I feel that I might as well have sat still waiting for the licking flames to reach the gas tank instead of grabbing the baby and running like hell to fall down on the desert and watch from the outside how the car rose and subsided?

It's hard to say. My mother would have a religious answer for this: God's will, we must accept it. And certainly this is the lesson that religion is so anxious to teach us, the mutability and irrelevance of all worldly possessions, all ties, all love. Every hand you hold will wither, the sun on your face will grow cold, the tender regard you feel or inspire, the passion, they will disappear and die. Children will read your letters and laugh. They will wear your clothes to masquerades. Your pictures will lie facedown in basements and attics.

Q: What about this, Mother, you optimist?

A: Better you should work hard and do for others. Why worry about what you can't help? Everybody dies.

Maybe that's it — what I want from her. The question: death. I remember the image I had of death when it first appeared to me and terrified me with its inevitability: the train that you could not get off. I couldn't get rid of it for a long time — the train would appear to me when I was going to sleep, in the shower, when I was walking to school. How did I get rid of it? I know I never discussed it with my mother.

Q: Is it fair to encourage anyone to take an interest, to be enthusiastic, to fall in love, to buy books, when we are going to die anyway?

She would sigh when I asked her this. She might answer with the story that is paired in my mind with the stolen-by-the-Gypsies story. The one about how, with so many to watch out for, ten children all rampaging about, demanding socks, dinner, getting into fights over whose turn to do chores, my grandmother forgot about her, about my mother. She fell asleep on the swing outside, and woke up to blackest night, crickets singing their cold song in her ear. She woke up under the cold stars outside in the dark, four years old, alone with herself.

And although on the face of it, the first story, the Aunt-Elizabeth-stolen-by-the-Gypsies story, is the happy-ending one, the reverse of bad fortune to good, the child restored to the bosom of her family, tears of grief turned to tears of joy — on second thought this one is better. It doesn't hold up a false picture of bliss forever; it promises nothing but a sort of survival, a going on in the dark, a long, long way.

A: Be quiet now, she'd say. You're upset over nothing.

My mother moves her hand, two of the fingers trembling independently of the others. What time is it? she asks. You ought to go home, have dinner. But I don't want to go just yet, and we start to gossip about the family. Who's having an operation, who's going to Sea World. My mother tells me about my niece's confirmation that I missed. She paints me a picture: the darkness, the bishop inviting the confirmees into the church, how they followed him in. The water he sprinkled in sharp little drops on the congregation — "should've worn a raincoat," my father said. The candles with little white paper cuffs, shining on the very young, velvety, dewy faces of girls dressed in red, white, pink, lace, silky dresses. The boys rougher, angular in suits, the music, the parents taking pictures, flash of the cameras. There was an old woman being received into the church and confirmed at the same time, who said the Apostles' Creed at the front of the church. (What does my mother mean by "an old woman"?)

It sounds very nice, I say, and think how if I were there I would have been teary, choked up, washed over with nostalgia for when I was Catholic, an embarrassment to all.

But the best thing, my mother says, wait, let me tell you. She puts her hand on my arm and I wait for more, more candleshine, more holy water.

There was this crazy old lady who came in, she says, with tiers of chiffon roses on her head like a crown and a sort of pillowcase for a veil, her white hair streaming down her back. She held herself like a queen. She sang all the songs and responses in a voice like a country-and-western singer. According to my mother it was ringing and true in the low and middle ranges, but cracked and strained at the top. You would have liked that, she says.

BRING BACK
THE DEAD

::

When Jenny's mother, Karen, was young, she and her sister had been telepathic with each other. They finished each other's sentences. They looked at each other across crowded rooms and knew what the other was thinking. With cards they were spectacular. On good days they might get 30, 35, 40 out of the deck. It had worked slightly better when Karen received, that is, sat with her eyes closed and waited to know what card her sister Laura was looking at. Their record was 41, on June 11, 1970, when Karen was thirteen and Laura was fourteen.

Now, thirty-two, Karen combs through her mind for those old skills, to hear, to see. She sits in a darkened room, having fasted, pure and clean — from a bath, from confession — and waits. Eyes closed, she tries to make a blank space in her mind, a place where something might enter. She tries to see a circle in the center of herself and herself sweeping, sweeping the thoughts that present themselves, out, out, away into the dark. The headline of today's newspaper, HAVE YOU SEEN THIS CHILD? Jenny. Stop, she says, stop. The snow, will it fall? Is it wet? Is it cold? Terry will have to shovel, his shovel digging deeper, deeper, stop, never mind. What am I wearing? She can't remember, can't feel her arms inside the sleeves, it doesn't matter. She feels cold with excitement for what might come, hot in the core of herself. Will she see something, or will it be instead a sure knowing? Will it be something heard, felt? Her fingers, moving in little scrabbling motions, feel only the cold soft skin of the leather couch. The ticking of the kitchen clock takes little chips out of time. She sees faces on the black wall behind her eyes, no one she knows, fading, stretching, whitening, sweep, sweep, clear it away . . .

"Karen."

She jerks, comes back. A shape in the darkness, a man. Terry.

"It's time for dinner," he says to her.

She stares at him. "Who are you?" she says to him. "I don't know you." She takes some pleasure in saying to him what is in her mind.

"You've got to stop. You've got to eat." He stands in front of her, his big hands hanging.

"I'll eat later. You go ahead."

"I'd like to eat with you, Karen."

"Maybe tomorrow. Tomorrow I'll make some meatloaf, I promise." She watches him to see if this will buy him off, make him go away.

"She's dead, Karen, she must be. You have to stop this."

"You want her to be dead."

"There's no point —"

"You don't want there to be a point."

She can hear him in the kitchen, opening the refrigerator door and closing it, picking up the phone, dialing, opening a pop-top can, his lowered voice speaking. She presses her head between her fists, but the space is gone, layered over with the motions and needs of the body. She has to go to the bathroom. "Bastard," she says, and then, raising her voice, "Son of a bitch."

....

When Terry goes she can only be relieved. It's temporary, he assures her, his car packed to the roof, nose pointed toward his mother's house. She holds his hand. "It's O.K.," she says.

She goes back into the house and sits at the kitchen table, a legal pad in front of her. When she hears the scraping sound his car makes backing out she picks up her pencil and starts to write. A list of things to do. A schedule for the day, for the night. She pours herself a cup of fresh coffee. The black liquid has a gleam on it, the cup is solid and heavy in her hand. The light from outside moves over her, a pattern of small shadows: the wind is moving the leaves of the tree, blocking and revealing the light from the sun.

She has decided against the psychic. No seance. These are options that have been offered to her in the weeks past. She has decided that these things would be wrong for her, for Jenny. It is her responsibility, she cannot turn to others. She will not pray. She will not upset, with outside intervention, the delicate balance of what is.

On the white of the paper she writes that she will clean the entire house very quickly, throw things out, anything damaged, anything old, anything that gives her a wrong feeling. In Jenny's room she will only dust, moving nothing, time enough to clean later. This is practical. The traces are there, she is the detective who will read them when she is fit.

"Four hours every day working."

She writes this and underlines it. This working is what she will be doing for Jenny. There is a list of duties she must fulfill, one by one, as she proceeds. She will get a job, part-time, an easy one, for money. She can't take the money she needs from Terry, this easy road is denied her. She unfolds the newspaper and spreads it out. With red ink she marks jobs that will do. No hesitation stays her hand, she doesn't worry about getting the job. She is owed everything now, people must allow her what she needs. They will part before her, they will buoy her up.

When Karen has filled the page with her writing, she gets up, leaving the pad and the pencil lined up on the bare table. She washes the cup, wipes it, puts it in the cupboard. She goes to the catch-all drawer and gets the scissors, the old ones, rusty along the cutting edges. They belonged to her mother. Holding them point down she goes to the bathroom and cuts her hair off.

....

She settles on the dining room, because of the size of the table, the largest flat space in the house. Here she can pile the newspapers she needs to look through, and the letters, which she keeps in stacks weighted down with rocks. The letters are from well-wishers, sympathizers, most of them from others to whom this has happened. There are some, unsigned, that accuse. The police have seen them, checked them out. Cranks, malcontents, twisted minds, cruel hearts, childless, or abandoned by their children, living in a dank, chill fog, breathing it in every day, spewing it back when they can. Karen has lived a long time in the world without knowing what it is like. But she reads them now, these letters, not as a penance, but for information, anything, an inflection, a misspelling, the way a letter is formed. The police don't know everything. She reads the letters of support the same way, for evil is a dissembler, the devil can smile. She spends an hour working with the papers every day.

She has other things she must do, like acknowledging all her faults, all the things she has done that she is being punished for. That she has thought too much about her body, her hair. That she has not fixed up the house, that she is not like other women. That she gets depressed. There are sexual faults as well, thinking about men, flirting in bars, divorcing her first husband for Terry, no wonder, it's no wonder. Karen is not so foolish as to think that Jenny is being withheld from her because of these things, all these things with which she reproaches herself. But she can see the need for control, for a single focus. She wants a whiteness, a wholeness, of mind and body. At night she lies flat on her back under the sheet and burns with it.

The evenings are bad, a slow waning of light and energy. She calls up people late at night and asks them to check on their children: Are they in their beds? Are they sick? Are they cold? — a duty, she thinks. Everyone should know all the time, keep it in their minds all the time. She started by going through the phone book alphabetically, but now it is random, she opens the book and runs her finger down the names. She keeps the names in a notebook so she doesn't call someone more than once, accidentally. These things take up her time.

She does not allow herself to smoke. The way the red eye

of the cigarette glows and pulses, the twisted, flattening curve of the smoke as it rises — anyone can see there's something wrong with it. But drinking is O.K. She drinks at night, after she is done working, her mind like a flat line, body slumped on the couch, her spine bent against it. Three shots, straight, sliding hot down her throat. She drinks them one careful sip at a time.

At night she dreams, dreams like this one which comes to her as a memory of someone else, a man who is remembering her, Karen, a girl who lived, like a princess, in a house with a tower, a tower with two rooms — one on each floor and a stairway that led up from a garden. In the dream that he is remembering, this strange man, the house with the tower is her grandma's house — in the same place, same street, the street with the police station on the corner (the man has to pass the police station, should they stop? the police would have axs, authority). The man who remembers is one of her two lovers or boyfriends — rivals. The scene he remembers is one where they are rushing there because they think Karen will kill herself. They come through gloom and darkening air, through the rose garden. The door is open, a big, heavy, glass-paneled door with a gathered curtain through which you can see dimly, but the man — who can he be with his big shoulders, his curly hair? — can't get in because his backpack gets in the way, he is stuck in the narrow door. "Push me through, Bob, push me through," he says. Bob, her other lover, the rival, is almost ready to climb over him, but the man who remembers is determined to be first. When he is through at last, just barely inside the door, he sees her, Karen, coming down the steps, in her robe, with a towel, she has been washing her hair and she is annoyed, she is not dead, not dying.

Karen doesn't understand this dream, she can't fit it in, though she tries because it is so clear, so full of some obscure significance. She lies in bed trying to think, wishing she still smoked. She never dreams of Jenny, and this upsets her. She tries to bring it on by thinking of her at night before she sleeps, trying to start off the dream as she used to when she was young, when she would think intensely of a boy she liked so she would dream about him.

She thinks:

. . . Jenny with her soft strands of hair falling over her neck and shoulders like a veil

. . . Jenny with her finger in her mouth sucking away the hurt from a burn

. . . Jenny sitting on her bed coloring in her coloring book, an activity she hid from her friends, too babyish, she strokes the crayons firmly along the heavy black curves that form the picture

. . . Jenny with her face turned up asking for milk apple juice a cookie

But it doesn't work. Karen dreams only stupid, useless dreams that make her angry if she remembers them.

In the morning she is up early, cutting bread from a home-made loaf sent by one of her neighbors. The knife is dull and it tears up the bread. The jagged, crumbling slices char when she tries to toast them, bright sparks fly up from the toaster. She picks the blackened wisps off as she eats, staring out at the sky, the trees.

She has to get ready to go to the job she has found, and

she goes upstairs to get dressed. Both the closets are hers now. She uses one for clothes for her job, the other for her working clothes, the clothes she wears at home to do her work for Jenny. She opens the working closet just to look, to let her eyes be cooled, soothed by the softness of them, the colors like clouds, like the ruffling leaves of trees, the linings of shells. All the other colors are in the job closet. She opens it and takes out a red skirt, a matching sweater. Some colors are not allowed at all: black, brown, a certain sickly rotting green. They went to Goodwill in a black plastic trash bag, enough of them to make it difficult to carry, she had to drag it out to the car, heave it into the trunk using the strength in her legs. She couldn't afford a muscle spasm. No injuries, no illness.

At her job, she lifts white squares of paper, uses them to pick up round, plump doughnuts and put them in crisp white bags or smooth white boxes that she assembles right in front of the customer. She wears a white smock to protect her clothes, pulls her hair back into a net. The teenagers who work with her laugh and talk all day long, they circle around her as if she were a rock, and she smiles to herself, for she feels so light, so transparent, a vessel of glass, filled, brimming. It is only the icing that bothers her, the chocolate, the sugar, maple, caramel, the sickly pink cherry glaze, the fluted dollops of whipped cream — no matter how careful she is, it gets on her hands, and on her forearms when she reaches into the display cases to get out three double chocolate, two sugar glaze, one jelly. She washes for a long time when she gets home, with strong oatmeal soap, scrubbing up to her elbows, rinsing, rinsing.

At home is better, cleaner. The house is attaining a bare,

an austere look. She is throwing things out, material things, those things she bought thoughtlessly, wanting them in a childish way, their bright colors, the smooth curves of the small appliances, the friendly, confiding brochures, the glittering bits of jewelry that she desired to hang around her neck, pinch onto her ears, the thick paperbacks, all of them with a man and a woman curving around each other, orchids nodding over their shoulders, ferns crushed beneath their feet. She is throwing these things out, plastic bags full. She watches the garbage men heave them, the great sodden lumps, dark and swollen, into their trucks. Or she is burning the things that will burn. She stands out in her yard behind the garage, her shoulders hunched inside her old coat, poking at the flames with a stick. A thin thread of smoke goes up. It is illegal, but her neighbors do not report her. Of course.

Back and forth.

To the job: the bath of the fluorescent lights, every surface sticky, the laughing secret faces of the teenagers, sallow under their hairnets, the anonymous white bags and boxes to be filled endlessly.

To the house: the increasing bareness, the smell of burning, the knives cutting up the endless bread from her neighbors, the ropes cutting cruelly into the bales of things she sends to Goodwill, the broken glass in the sink she cuts her finger on, the knives, the burning, the ropes, the silence, the silence.

She still sees people. The police. A few of the volunteer workers who looked for Jenny come by sometimes. She offers them coffee, although she drinks none herself, nor does she eat any of the doughnuts she arranges on an old plastic plate, a mound of them, shit-brown chocolate, éclairs filled with oozing yellow custard. She can bring home a free dozen a week, and her employer urges her to take more, more. He fills her arms with doughnuts when she leaves, his sad eyes moving over her face. The ones that the visitors don't eat, she puts out in the yard for the birds. The grass is dotted with doughnuts, pecked into pieces.

When they are gone, the police with their charts and forms, the volunteers with their soft voices, she goes upstairs, she ascends through her house, feet echoing on the bare wood of the stairs, the uncarpeted hall. She goes into Jenny's room. She closes the door and sits, not on the bed, never the bed, on the desk chair which she pulls out and places in the center of the room. She sits there, back straight, feet flat on the floor. She takes off her shoes so she can feel the rug under her feet, the only rug left in the house, pink, soft, fluffy. She sits and holds an object, a different one every night. Jenny's alarm clock. Jenny's pencil with the dinosaur eraser. Jenny's rain hat. One of her bedroom slippers. Her old doll. Her gymnastics trophy, her initial necklace, her math notebook. She holds them in both hands, eyes closed, for as long as seems right, and she waits. Jenny's tortoiseshell barrette. Jenny's pink heart pillow. Jenny's Chap Stick: she opens it up and touches it to her lips, but does not rub. Jenny's unwashed nightgown. Jenny's geode: she grinds her hand into its little mouth, scrapes her knuckles raw against the sharp little teeth of its crystals.

She needs to sleep less and less, which is O.K., is fine. But the nights are so long. There are times she can't work, when it feels wrong, Jenny's room is closed to her. There is nothing more to throw out. She has sifted and sifted the piles of letters and clippings on the dining-room table and now they are useless, drifts of paper with dead black letters imprisoned on them. One night when Karen stalks the bare floors of the dark house, the moon is shining through the curtainless windows. She can see the dark squatting shapes of the neighbors' houses, all the lights turned out, except maybe the high dim square of the bathroom where the light is left on in case someone wants to go in the middle of the night, in case someone wants a drink of water, has had a nightmare, something bad was coming, something bad was seeping under the door, flooding the unlit corners of the bedroom, living in the closet, taking up all the air, something's fingers pressing on their small throats, touching pushing probing their small bodies — Karen hangs on to the window frame, tearing at the wood with her nails, holding on to the noise in her body, gulping it down, closing her lips tight.

When she can move, she turns on all the lights from the basement up to the attic. But when she comes back into the living room, it's not enough, so she turns on the radio as well, and sits down on the couch, drawing her knees up against her body. She listens carefully to a commercial for a rock concert, one for a feminine deodorant. A man's voice comes on, deep and scratchy, and she listens to that, he is talking to people who call in to talk about what? — who is running for president, response times for police and emergency calls, a local bank scandal. "Call up, folks," he says in his thick, deep voice. "Let us know what's on your mind."

It is such a relief to talk. Karen can feel the hard wild noise in her body flowing away as she talks, her lips against the phone receiver, she can feel the buzz of her words escaping. She knows not to talk too long. She calls only when she has to, when that pressure of sound pushes too hard from inside. She calls different numbers, radio hosts and TV talk shows.

She tells parts of her story, sometimes using different names, or she makes up things that might have happened.

"You don't know what a relief it is to talk to you, Joe, Geraldo, Oprah," she says, holding the phone with both hands. When she is talking to them, she calls Jenny "my little girl."

"My little girl is twelve," she says. "We've had a lot of trouble with her. She goes to the mall, she wants a boyfriend."

"My little girl had a bad experience. It was the janitor at her school. Should we send her for counseling?"

The advice she receives, the solemn precepts of the talk show's guest experts, the applause of the sympathetic audience, they roll over her like balm, like the healing waters of Jordan, and she can lie back, she can sleep. If she sleeps on the couch it is O.K., it is friendly to know that she is in the middle of the house, in all the light, all the heated empty air.

She has to stop though, because Terry finds out. He comes over, and although she will not open the door to him, she can hear anyway through the heavy wood, the double-glass storm door.

"You have to stop," he says. "Please stop. I can't stand it."

She hears a thump, imagines his head banging against the door, and she allows her own head to fall forward, resting lightly against the smooth, white-painted wood.

"I heard you on the radio, I knew it was you," he says. "I can't stand it. Don't you think I'm dying, too?"

He sends a priest the next day. She invites him in and they sit in the living room, he on the couch, she on the old armchair. He asks her for some water, and she brings it to him in a white plastic glass that is ringed by dancing girls with big bonneted heads who carry basketball-sized strawberries. It belonged to Jenny, she tells him before he can begin to talk to her. She'd had it for some time, had maybe gotten too old for it but she still liked it for her orange juice.

The priest nods, quick little jabs of his head, all the time Karen is speaking. When she stops, he asks if she has been going to church.

"Oh, yes," she says. She inclines her head when she says it, lowering her eyes, as if thinking of the comfort of the mass. She has not been to church for years, doesn't he know that, is he so stupid?

Perhaps she's lonely, he says, hunching his shoulders awkwardly, in this big house. What about her family? her parents? any sisters or brothers? The comfort of family in hard times . . .

"There's no one." She smiles so he will know she doesn't mind.

He thought a sister, he says, passing the glass from one hand to the other.

"Oh, no." She thinks of Laura, across the country, imagines her reading about Jenny in the papers, biting the corner off her toast triangle, her glasses slipping down her nose. "No," she says. There was no reason for Laura to come, she has told her not to come.

He goes away. She stands on the front porch, her arms folded across her chest, and watches him get into his car. If she were a mean person, she might take note of how new his car is. How can he have this new shiny-black car when he serves God? He hasn't drunk any of his water, when he left he set the full glass on the floor beside the couch, and Karen leaves it there until the water evaporates, sucked into the air.

She stops calling the radio and the TV, though. And it's all right, really, it was a distraction, a vanity, a soft shirking comfort.

....

She thinks of this as phase two, or sometimes just the next part. Her new face is smooth. She answers questions in a steady voice. Smooth, like a skin of latex paint. Not cheerful, she knows not to be cheerful. She goes to the grocery store, moves through the aisles holding her face up, tilted just slightly to the left as if she is going to ask a question. To the drugstore, the gas station. Everyone can see that she is all right, her clothes are unwrinkled, her shoes match, her hair is combed. The corners of her mouth are turned down, a tiny graceful curve that she has practiced in the bathroom mirror. And she lies, she lies all the time. She says that she is getting help, of course, she is seeing someone who was recommended to her, and it is worth it though it is so expensive. That she and Terry of course still love each other but the strain drove them apart, but maybe that marriage just wasn't meant to be. That she is starting to put her life back together. That if only some good can come out of all this, she will feel better, if some other child, some other mother does not have to suffer. People tell her how nice her hair looks, or say how her hair used to look so nice when it was long. When someone says to her that she is young, she will be able to have other children, she nods her head, nods, nods, nods, as if she is driving a nail in with the bones of her skull.

At home, she works in a frenzy. She drops her purse by the door when she comes in, goes straight to Jenny's room,

stays there for hours some nights, sitting upright in the chair,
or moving around the perimeter of the walls, touching the
knob on the closet door, the tip of the bedpost, the cool
smooth glass of the mirror. She would like to cry sometimes,
to scream. Where are you, where are you? Answer me this
minute. Her face in the mirror remains blank, unrippled. She
smooths her hair over her ears, rounding it to the shape of
her cheeks. She goes downstairs to look for more things to
burn. Standing over the fire, she crosses her arms over her
heart. The smoke twisting up, the sharp orange flames, like
little knives. The blackened patch in the grass is like her
friend.

When the police come again, she puts her face between
herself and their blue bodies, for she can't allow them to tell
her certain things. She holds herself so that she can go away
if she has to, leaving her face behind to gawp and stretch and
moan. But they have not come to tell her that.

They think someone has seen Jenny. They think. Someone
has seen a girl who looked like Jenny. Who might have been
Jenny. This person, a woman, wondered at the time if everything was all right, thought of calling the police, but didn't
know if she should. But now she has. The police are cautious,
cautiously optimistic, one of them says. When they go away,
Karen stands for a minute, pressing her hands against her
thighs. She goes into the living room and picks up the glass
that the priest left next to the couch, takes it into the kitchen,
and puts it on the drainboard.

Now Karen has to watch the news, read the newspapers,
which she hasn't been doing. She wears headphones at her
job so she can hear the hourly news reports. Her employer,

the manager of the doughnut shop, questions her with his eyes whenever their paths cross, and she allows her mouth to droop into its curve so that he will go away.

She stays out of Jenny's room. She huddles on the couch, piles of newspapers slipping from the cushions. She steps carefully so that they won't slide under her feet on the bare wood floor. Terry comes over with a bucket of fried chicken. She gets out plates, forks, knives, and they sit across from each other at the kitchen table, each with a piece of chicken on their plate at which they jab with their forks. Terry smokes. He has started again, he tells her, although his mother hates the smell. He lists for Karen the different room deodorizer sprays his mother has tried without success. His mother's arthritis is worse, he tells her. When he leaves he grabs her by the elbows, pulling her against his chest, kisses her, and she does not resist, but it is like two pieces of wood coming together, the union of slabs of concrete, of frozen lumps of earth.

How long does this last, this stiff time, this time of waiting? Not long enough.

On March 24 the fields around the town are thawing, runnels of water flowing in the ditches. Karen is at work, sliding her sticky arms in and out of the shelves of doughnuts. She no longer wears her headphones, though she still carries the radio in the pocket of her white smock. She moves dozens of doughnuts from the shelves to the bags, to the boxes, nesting them carefully in the white paper squares, chocolate, cherry, coconut, Dutch apple. When her shift is over, she hangs her smock up, walks on her ordinary feet to her car. She gets in, starts it, puts her hands on the wheel, sighs. She is tired, she closes her eyes. When she opens them, she sees the manager at the door of the doughnut shop. He is looking at her, he is opening the door. He is walking toward her, slow, one hand outstretched. He looks wrong, he ought to be waving, smiling, wiping tears of emotion from the corners of his eyes. The car is already started, she says to herself, she can gun the motor until it roars, let the car leap forward, run him down. But when she puts it into drive, she swerves around him, a quick neat curve. She drives up and down the streets, up and down, past the grocery store, the drugstore. She drives slowly and deliberately past the school playground, sliding her eyes over its smooth concrete. She drives to the mall, which she hasn't seen for months, and circles it, driving crossways in the parking lot, ducking through the middle of the aisles. She drives out into the country, going straight like an arrow, passing whatever appears in front of her. She doesn't turn on the radio. She thinks, and her thoughts are light, they rise and drift away from her, out the windows of the car into the damp spring air.

When it has been long enough, she goes home. She parks down the block, goes through the night like a shadow, slipping though her neighbors' yards to spy on her own house. It is dark, safe. Inside, she leans her back against the front door, breathing hard and deep. She is gathering her forces, she has known all along what she had to do, what would be the right thing that would bring Jenny back, she knew it, she knew it. But something held her back, cowardice, a fear that she would use it and it would turn out to be wrong. Now she is sure.

But first she goes through the dark house, she fills everything capable of holding liquid with water: bowls, pans, cups, vases, buckets, the sinks, the bathtub, an eye cup, the roasting pan. She turns off the electricity and lights candles: white or off-white, all scents, vanilla, lily of the valley, coconut. She sets them on the tables, on the floors, the counters, moving quickly, deliberately.

The phone is ringing, but she does not hear.

Upstairs in Jenny's room, she opens Jenny's jewelry box, blue with a ballerina who rises with the middle tier, her skirt like a cloud, and she takes out Jenny's locket. She presses the catch with her thumb, but doesn't open it, not yet. She knows what is supposed to be inside, a picture of Karen, a picture of Terry. She holds it between her two hands, the chain dangling down from her clasped palms. She stands there holding it, feeling the house around her, dark, in every room, the flickering points of fire, the glistening surfaces of the water. This is the thing, she knows. Her eyes are closed, the lids jumping with her pulse, and when she opens them, she will see, she will know.

She waits for an emptiness in her mind, until the ringing of the telephone is like a slow beat of music, she waits for something to come rushing toward her, feels the breath of it against the skin of her face, the small, the infinitesimal movement of the universe that will bring Jenny back to her. It is so easy, she says, eyes closed. It will be so easy, this, the last thing that will bring her to life, her mother looking in a mirror, candles lit, her clean brushed hair hanging thin around her face. The phone is ringing, ringing, and she feels the taut surfaces of the water in the bowls, the cups, the glasses, wrinkle and ripple, the water sliding, sloshing, the flames of the candles flickering, wavering, their small lights dying away to blue points. What is it, she cries out, what is it?

Water is sliding down over her face, drops of water, her

tears, and she knows already, will not let herself know that her daughter is dead. I'll do anything, she says, clenching her eyes closed.

What would she do to get her back? What or who would she sacrifice? Her own life, health, happiness — yes, of course, yes. But if Jenny is dead? Could she bring her back, send someone in her stead? Someone else's husband, wife, someone else's child? Yes, she says. Yes, I could. And on the inside of her eyes, she sees, coming from far away, a child, a girl, blond Jenny, coming back with streaks of mud on her face and leaves caught in her hair, her clothes stained, torn. She takes in all the parts of her, Jenny's brown eyes, her hair in great loops and snarls, the smear of leaf mold on her arms, the earth under her bitten fingernails, closer, closer, the crumbled bit of leaf caught in the soft hair just by her ear, the streaks of dirt on her cheeks and her forehead, the rip in the shoulder of her yellow T-shirt, the mud on the toes of her sneakers, the earth at the corners of her mouth, her hair, her eyes, her hands, her mouth —

No, she screams, no, and she drops the locket, she falls to the floor, she lies down and grinds her face into the carpet. Jenny is dead, she says, Jenny is dead.

....

In the morning, Terry and his mother and Karen's sister Laura come and get her, they find her in the house among the guttering blackened candles, the silent pools of water. They lead her out of the house, and she lets them. When they go through the kitchen she sees that water has run out of the refrigerator, making a puddle of discolored liquid on the floor.

Leaning back against the seat in the car, Karen allows Laura to take her hand. She lets the trees, the houses slide past her eyes. They will do what is necessary, they will talk to the police, the press, to each other. They will go to the funeral, will see Jenny lying, like Snow White, in a glass box, they will be cold, with the dead traces of tears on their cheeks.

And she thinks, as the sun shines in the pale-blue sky, and the car slices through the thick, clear air, she imagines lost opportunities. Oh, to undo things. Oh, that we would never do or not do the things we will regret forever. She lifts her hand to her heart under the cover of her coat.

She knows she will be constantly on the alert for the rest of her life, she swears it, running her eyes over every child she sees. Does he look scared? mistreated? is there the shadow of a bruise by her eye, on his wrist? Does the man with her pull her roughly by her arm? Does he hardly dare to raise his eyes or head? Is her hair dull, her skin pale from a diet of fast food? Are they all right? Are they in danger? Are they an hour or a day away from death?

ABOUT THE AUTHOR

MARY GRIMM was born in Cleveland, Ohio, where she has lived most of her life. She was managing editor of *The Gamut* at Cleveland State University before joining the faculty of Case Western Reserve University in 1989 to teach creative writing. Her fiction has been published in *Redbook* and *The New Yorker*. Her short story "We" won a National Magazine Award for *The New Yorker* in 1988 and was also selected by *Best American Short Stories* as one of the hundred most distinguished short stories of 1988.

ABOUT THE TYPE

This book was set in Berling. Designed in 1951 by Karl Erik Forsberg for the Typefoundry Berlingska Stilgjuteri AB in Lund, Sweden; it was released the same year in foundry type by H. Berthold AG. A classic oldface design, its generous proportions and inclined serifs make it highly legible.